SECOND chances

a holiday romance

Cover images by:
© Period Images
stock.adobe.com
© ekostsov
© Timmary
© boroboro
Cover design by: T.M. Franklin

$\mathcal{E}$nchanted

PUBLICATIONS
www.enchantedpublications.com
ISBN-13: 978-0-9985468-6-5
ISBN-10: 0-9985468-6-0
Visit the Author's web site at
www.TMFranklin.com

SUMMARY

Sometimes second chances aren't quite what you expect.

Every Christmas Eve, Carter Reed sits in a bar and regrets the decision he made ten years earlier that tore the love of his life from him. Mackenzie Monroe was his everything, but he left her behind to follow his dreams.

Now those dreams all revolve around her. The one who got away.

Or so he thinks.

A not-so-chance encounter with a mysterious stranger sends Carter on a mystical journey to fix the mistakes of the past. But he quickly finds out making things right isn't as simple as making a different choice.

Second Chances is a story about a man who gets a peek at what his life could be, if only he'd walked a different path. In the tradition of It's a Wonderful Life and A Christmas Carol, it's a heartwarming romance sprinkled with a touch of magic that's sure to become a holiday favorite.

SECOND

chances

a holiday romance

chapter
ONE

city sidewalks,
busy sidewalks

Snow fell softly on the New York City streets as people rushed here and there trying to get to Christmas Eve festivities, wives gripping their husbands' arms to avoid slipping on the icy sidewalk. Down the street, a man in a Santa suit stood next to a Salvation Army bucket, haphazardly ringing a bell. Teenage boys, who had snuck out after dark, laughed and threw snowballs while trading sips from a bottle of vodka swiped from a father's liquor cabinet.

Carter Reed saw none of it.

He sat at a nondescript bar, as he had every Christmas Eve for the past ten years. Different cities. Different bars. The same memories.

He frowned at his distorted reflection in the mirror behind the bar, swirling his drink idly, before taking a sip with a slight grimace.

"Mind if I sit here?" A pretty young woman with pink hair appeared in the mirror beside him, but Carter didn't turn to face her. He shrugged in response and watched her reflection distractedly as she climbed onto the stool to his right. She was tall, almost as tall as him, he'd guess, and her curly hair varied in shade from the barest hint of pink at the roots to almost fuchsia at the ends brushing her shoulders. Her skin was pale, cheeks flushed and her eyes a vivid blue. The color combination reminded him of cotton candy . . . or unicorns. Next to her, he looked monochromatic, his own dark blond hair and black jacket making his skin look almost gray in comparison.

She smiled at him in invitation. "Sure is cold," she said as she tugged off a pair of leather gloves. "Thought I'd stop in here to warm up. Oh!" She looked up at the TV in the corner and her smile widened as she slipped out of her coat, laying it on the stool beside her. "I love this movie!"

Carter followed her gaze, recognizing a familiar scene from *It's a Wonderful Life*. George Bailey was about to jump from the bridge, in the hopes that his life insurance would pay off his family's debt. Carter watched in silence as Clarence—the angel sent to save George's life—beat him to the punch and plunged into the icy water.

"I watch it every year, and it still makes me cry," the woman said quietly, propping her elbows on the bar.

Carter nodded slightly and swallowed the rest of his drink, rolling an ice cube around his mouth once before letting it plop back into the glass.

"I'm Tess," she said tentatively, a little put off by Carter's indifferent demeanor.

Carter took a breath and forced a slight smile, not wanting to offend her. She seemed nice enough. It wasn't her fault he was in a terrible mood and intent on wallowing in that mood for the rest of the night.

"Carter," he said finally, catching the bartender's attention and lifting his empty glass. The bartender nodded and Carter pointed to Tess, indicating he should bring her a drink as well. Evidently, Tess was a regular, because the bartender didn't ask what she wanted, but delivered a clear drink in a tumbler along with Carter's whiskey.

"Thanks," she said with a smile, sipping her drink.

"Gin and tonic?" Carter asked.

"Vodka Collins," Tess replied, running her finger around the rim of the glass. "So . . . Carter . . . you on your way to a party?" She glanced down at the engraved invitation lying on the bar next to a thick, hardback book.

Her book.

Carter took another gulp of his drink. "Decided not to go," he said shortly.

Unthwarted, Tess persisted. "Yeah," she said, "I can see where a dim and dusty bar would hold much more appeal than a big, glamorous charity party at . . ." She glanced at the invitation again and smirked slightly. ". . . the Hotel Martienne."

Carter said nothing.

"Wait a second, the Martienne?" Tess continued. "I read about that in the paper. Isn't Mackenzie Monroe supposed to be there?"

3

Carter cringed slightly, hearing her name spoken aloud.

"Yeah . . ." Tess reached for the book, flipping it over so she could see the cover. "Oh wow—I love *Cold Winter Nights*! The whole *Nights* series is amazing," she said, her own excitement making her oblivious to Carter's discomfort.

"Mackenzie Monroe is my favorite author," she gushed. "They were giving away a couple tickets to the party on the radio, but I couldn't get through. I can't believe you have an invitation and you're not going!"

Tess paused, and Carter fought a heavy sigh, knowing she was hoping he would give her his invitation, or at least ask her to go along. He glanced at her in the mirror. She was flipping through his copy of *Cold Winter Nights* with a smile on her face. He'd intended to go. To finally see Kenzie . . . speak to her. He'd ducked into the bar only to garner a little liquid courage.

He was still waiting for that courage to kick in.

It had been ten long years since he made the biggest mistake of his life. He'd had the ring in his pocket, but at the last minute opted to give Kenzie the silver bracelet he'd purchased as a backup Christmas gift instead. She'd smiled and thanked him, of course, but it was just a few days later that they had The Talk.

The *Do We Have a Future?* Talk.

The *Are We Moving Forward?* Talk.

The *Will You Commit to Me or Leave Me Behind When You Take That Internship in New York?* Talk.

4

He'd let her go. He said he wasn't ready and Kenzie's eyes had filled with tears. He'd left her behind, moved to New York, and tried not to look back.

But on Christmas Eve, looking back was all he could do. The what-ifs just about drove him crazy, and instead of missing her less with each passing year, he found he actually missed her more. In the early years, he'd picked up the phone a hundred times to call her, but shame and guilt kept him from dialing her number. Plus, there was the fact that nothing had really changed. He was still in New York, pursuing a career in television journalism. She was still in grad school in Seattle, and from what little he'd heard from mutual friends, she'd moved on.

He hadn't. He tried dating, but never really connected with anyone. He tried one-night stands, but found them unfulfilling. So he focused on his career, working long hours, moving up the ladder, and trying not to think about what he'd left behind.

It only got worse when Kenzie's first novel hit the New York Times Bestseller list . . . as did her second. Soon, her picture was in every bookstore . . . on TV commercials . . . her glowing brown eyes seemed to surround him, watching his every move.

It was torture.

So when the network offered him a foreign correspondent position, he'd jumped at the chance. He traveled the world, reporting on wars, famine, drugs, politics . . . and spent as little time in the United States as possible. He lived out of a worn duffle bag, roaming from disaster to tragedy, and avoiding civilization as much as he could. But now, after six years on the road, he'd been given the opportunity for a special weekly segment on the nightly news. It was an offer too good to pass up, but it meant less time out of the country. He came back to New York to meet with his executive producer and found out all of the senior management and on-air talent had been invited to a charity party.

Where Mackenzie Monroe was to be the guest of honor.

To see her name printed on the invitation was jarring, to say the least. In that moment, he decided he was going to go to that party and see her. Say hello, and finally lay the past to rest. He'd even bought a copy of her latest book so he'd have a reason to approach her.

He'd already read it, of course—numerous times. He always snagged a copy of her books as soon as they were released and devoured them quickly, straining to find a glimpse of who Kenzie had become in the printed lines. His own copy of *Cold Winter Nights* was dog-eared and cracked, the dust cover torn from his repeated readings. Tess was right—the book was amazing.

"Carter?" Tess's voice made him realize he'd been staring off into space. "You okay?"

Carter sucked an ice cube out of his drink and crunched it slowly. "Yeah. Just thinking."

"Want to talk about it?"

Carter shrugged.

"Might help," she suggested.

He considered Tess's offer. For some reason, he liked her . . . felt he could trust her. He'd just met her, but she almost felt like a friend, and the truth was, he had very few of those. Carter's tongue was also a little loose, given the whiskey he'd had, and he thought it might be nice to have someone to talk to.

Oh, why not? He was in a wallowing mood. Might as well add whining to the equation. Carter reached for the invitation, running his fingers over the engraved lettering, before tapping it against the bar lightly.

"I was actually on my way to the party when I stopped in here," he said finally.

Tess sipped her drink. "And . . ." she prodded.

Carter exhaled heavily before he continued, ". . . and, I just can't bring myself to get up and go."

"What's stopping you?"

Carter grimaced slightly. "Kenzie."

"Kenzie?" she repeated slowly before her mouth dropped open. "You mean Mackenzie Monroe? You know her?"

"I did. It was a long time ago." His eyes focused on Kenzie's name in gold, sparkling script on the invitation.

Tess studied him for a moment before she nodded slowly in understanding. "I should have known."

Carter turned to her in curiosity. "Known what?"

"Haven't you heard?" she replied wryly. "All the good ones are either married or gay . . . or still in love with the one that got away."

7

Carter flushed slightly. "Is it that obvious?"

"Only to an extremely gifted judge of character."

Carter chuckled.

"I never thought a guy who dodges grenades for a living would be such a chicken," Tess teased.

Carter's eyes widened. "How did you know—"

Tess waved a hand before picking up her drink again. "It took me a minute to place the face, but I do watch the news." She rolled her eyes at his shocked look. "Don't worry. Your secret's safe with me, Carter. But seriously, this is obviously killing you. Don't you want to at least *try* to see her?"

Carter swallowed down the rest of his drink, a warm numbness finally drifting from his stomach to his extremities. Of course he wanted to see her . . . needed to see her.

He could do this.

Taking a deep breath, he offered Tess a shaky smile. "Want to go to a party?"

chapter TWO

silver bells

C arter felt the nausea set in as they headed for the Hotel Martienne, each passing block adding to the lump of anxiety in the pit of his stomach.

"You okay?" Tess's worried gaze proved his inner turmoil was more than evident on his face.

He shrugged. "Yeah. I just . . . what if she hates me?" he murmured quietly.

To her credit, Tess didn't try to gloss over Carter's concerns. "Maybe she will," she said bluntly, "but isn't it better to know for sure? It's pretty obvious you can't move on with your life without knowing for certain that it's over with her.

"And there's always the chance that she misses you as much as you miss her," she pointed out with a light touch on his arm. "That's worth the risk, don't you think?"

Carter nodded, his swallow sticking in his throat as he turned to look out the window. The cab pulled up in front of the hotel and with a deep

breath, Carter got out, turning to offer his hand to
Tess as she alighted.

"Here goes nothing," he said with a weak grin
as he released her hand.

Tess patted her hair. "Are you sure I look
okay?" She'd insisted they stop at her apartment so
she could at least change into a dress and freshen
her makeup. Her cotton candy hair was swept up in
a fifties-style roll and dangly earrings sparkled as
she moved.

"You look fine," he said, then quickly added, "I
mean . . . *great.*"

Tess tossed her head. "Sweet talker," she
replied. "Come on. Let's go get your girl."

They walked across the hotel lobby, and Carter
barely noticed the three-story-high grand columns
sweeping upward to the backlit onyx ceiling. Tess,
however, took it all in with wide eyes—from the
marble floor to the twenty-four-foot Christmas tree
decorated with twinkling lights and sparkling
ornaments.

"This is incredible," she murmured, but Carter
didn't hear her. His eyes were on the entrance to
Monique's, the restaurant off the hotel lobby where
the party was being held. He felt Tess take his
hand, squeezing it in encouragement before letting
it go as they walked into the restaurant and he
handed his invitation to a man at the door. He
gripped his copy of Kenzie's book tightly as his
eyes adjusted to the dim interior. The only light in
the spacious room came from the candles on the
tables and the thousands of twinkling Christmas
lights entwined in the room's trademark Acacia

trees. Carter couldn't focus on the atmosphere, however. His eyes scanned the room anxiously, searching for the face that had haunted his dreams for years . . . Hell, for as long as he could remember.

Then he saw her.

She was standing on the opposite side of the room, her face glowing as she smiled at the people around her. She was wearing a black cocktail dress, shot through with some kind of silver thread that caught the light, causing her to almost sparkle under the twinkling trees. Carter's eyes drank in her form, sliding down her body to take in the long legs peeking out from the short hem of the dress, and the teetering heels she never would have worn when he knew her.

She laughed, and Carter's breath caught.

Even over the voices in the crowded room, he recognized her familiar tinkling laughter and his gaze shot to her face to see sparkling eyes and a light flush staining her cheeks. If Kenzie ten years before was pretty . . . gorgeous, even . . . *this* Kenzie was breathtaking—her natural beauty heightened by the confidence of a woman who'd come into her own.

If Carter had any doubts before that moment that he was still in love with her, they were obliterated.

He was lost.

"Are you just going to stand here staring at her?" Tess whispered, elbowing him lightly. Carter jumped slightly at the intrusion into his little Kenzie bubble.

He cleared his throat. "No. I'm going," he said, grabbing a couple of champagne flutes from the tray of a passing waiter. He handed one to Tess and drained his own in a couple of quick gulps before squaring his shoulders and turning to walk toward Kenzie. He took one step and stopped in his tracks.

A tall, dark-haired man approached Kenzie, handing her a drink and placing his hand on the small of her back possessively. She smiled up at him and sipped her champagne as he leaned in and kissed her cheek softly. They turned together to talk to the couple in front of them and again, Kenzie laughed at something one of them had said. She leaned slightly into the man's body, and Carter felt his blood heat.

Who was that?

Unconsciously, he took a few steps backward.

"Carter?" Tess was watching him warily. "What are you doing?"

"I can't . . ." Carter shook his head slowly. "I've got to go."

"Don't you want to talk to her?"

"I can't," he repeated, his eyes still focused on the man who'd apparently replaced him.

Tess looked longingly toward Kenzie. "Okay . . . we can go," she said quietly. "If you're sure . . ."

"No, it's fine." Carter thrust his book into Tess's hands. "Take this. Go get an autograph. Have fun."

"Carter, I don't need to . . ."

"No, it's okay," he stammered. "I just need to be alone. You've been great . . . have a good time, okay?"

12

Not waiting for her response, Carter turned on his heel and practically ran out of the restaurant and across the lobby, only stopping once he'd emerged onto the snow-covered sidewalk. He pulled his coat tightly around him and turned to the left, not sure where he was headed.

She'd moved on.

He'd lost his chance.

He'd lost her.

He'd lost her.

The reality hit him like a ton of bricks. Over the years he'd held on to the hope that someday they'd find their way back to each other. Somehow, once they'd done what they needed to do, they'd have their second chance.

But no.

No. It was over.

He huddled in his coat, his head down as he stomped through the snow, his mind swimming with the lost opportunities . . . his heart breaking all over again.

Carter had no idea how long he wandered the wintry streets, avoiding eye contact with anyone he encountered, and ignoring the happy sounds of Christmas around him. A passing car hit a slushy puddle, splashing icy water up his leg and Carter barely noticed.

She was gone.

Gone.

He was such an idiot. If only he'd had an ounce of courage, he'd have proposed ten years ago. They'd be together today. He'd be the one with his hand at her back. He'd be the one bringing her champagne and making her laugh.

He'd be the one loving her . . . being loved by her.

The sound of angry voices brought Carter out of his bout of self-loathing. He looked up and realized he had arrived back at the bar where he'd started off the evening. A group of men hovered in the shadows of an alley next to the bar, and it took a moment for Carter to comprehend what was happening. Two large men dressed in black were standing over another, smaller man cowering on the ground. As Carter watched, one of the men pulled his leg back and kicked the smaller one in the stomach. The man cried out in pain, clutching his abdomen.

"Hey!" Carter called out on instinct. "Hey! What do you think you're doing?"

The men turned to him, and to Carter's surprise, took off running down the alley. Carter hurried over to the man on the ground, glancing up to see the attackers had disappeared around the corner. He crouched down over the victim.

"Are you all right?" he asked, reaching for his cell phone. "Don't move. I'll call an ambulance . . . and the police."

"No. It's all right," the man said, sitting up and running his hands through his hair and over his rumpled shirt. "I'm fine. You scared them off before they could really hurt me."

Carter watched the man warily as he stood up. "Are you sure? That big guy kicked you pretty hard."

The man grinned and patted his stomach. "I'm tougher than I look," he replied.

Carter hoped so, because the guy didn't look tough at all. Fair-haired and baby-faced, he seemed young, but for some reason his blue eyes had an air of wisdom that made Carter believe he was older than he thought. He was dressed in a white shirt and faded blue jeans—no coat—and Carter was surprised to find there was not a speck of dirt on him.

Weird.

"I'm Henry," he said with a smile, holding out his hand. Carter shook it gently.

"Carter," he replied automatically. "Are you sure you're okay?"

Henry waved a hand. "I'm fine, thanks to you. Not a lot of people would have intervened in a situation like that."

Carter shrugged, a little embarrassed by the praise. "I'm sure anyone would have."

"You don't know people like I know people." Henry looked up at the neon sign in the bar window. "Can I buy you a drink? It's the least I can do."

Carter started to refuse. The last thing he needed was more alcohol in his depressed state. But Henry was watching him with such a look of gratitude and enthusiasm, he found himself accepting the offer.

They walked into the dimly lit bar and Carter took a seat on the same stool he'd had before. Henry sat down next to him and held up a finger to the bartender, ordering two whiskeys on the rocks.

Carter blinked in surprise that the guy would know his drink of choice.

Henry grinned. "Lucky guess," he said. "So, Carter," he continued, ignoring Carter's mystified expression. "What are you doing wandering around the city streets on Christmas Eve? Don't you have somewhere to be?"

Carter took a gulp of his drink, relishing in the burn as it made its way to his stomach. "Nope."

"No? Me neither. Just hanging out, enjoying the atmosphere," Henry said brightly.

Carter raised an eyebrow. "Didn't look like you were enjoying it much."

Henry shrugged. "Oh, well . . . that's in the past. No point in dwelling on it," he replied cheerfully, swirling the ice in his own drink. He had yet to take a sip of it, and when he noticed Carter had already drained his, he slid it across the bar to him. "Help yourself," he said. "I'm not really much of a drinker."

Carter nodded in thanks and lifted the glass to his lips. He absently noticed familiar dialogue coming from the TV above the bar and looked up to see the same scene from *It's a Wonderful Life* playing again—when George was about to jump from the bridge. Carter assumed they were running a Christmas Eve marathon or something.

"Great movie," Henry said quietly.

Carter just drank his whiskey, letting the cool liquid warm in his mouth before trailing down his throat. He could feel the slight numbness move through his body, slowing his movements and relaxing his muscles. He watched the old black and white movie silently, listening to the familiar lines.

"I'm worth more dead than alive," George *lamented.*

"Now look, you mustn't talk like that," the angel, Clarence, *said reproachfully. "I won't get my wings with that attitude. You just don't know all that you've done. If it hadn't been for you . . ."*

George interrupted, "Yeah, if it hadn't been for me, everybody'd be a lot better off . . ."

"Sad, isn't it?" Henry drew Carter's attention. "To be so full of regret."

Carter said nothing. The warmth of the room combined with the whiskey caused him to sway slightly on his stool, his eyes still focused on the screen.

"So you still think killing yourself would make everyone happier, eh?" Clarence asked.

"Oh, I don't know," George admitted. *"I guess you're right. I suppose it would have been better if I'd never been born at all."*

"You ever feel like that, Carter?" He turned to see Henry studying him intently.

"Like I want to kill myself?" Carter scoffed. "No."

"No, that's not what I meant," Henry replied softly. "I meant, have you ever felt like you've failed? Like if you could go back and do things over again, you'd make different choices?"

Carter shrugged, draining his glass. "Who hasn't?"

"What would you change, Carter?" Henry asked as Carter squirmed slightly under his

17

scrutiny. "If you could fix one mistake in your past, what would it be?"

Carter considered the question for a moment. He didn't know why he felt compelled to answer such a personal question posed by a stranger. Perhaps it was the alcohol . . . or the emotional turmoil of the evening. Maybe he was just feeling sorry for himself. Whatever the reason, he found himself saying just one word.

"Kenzie."

Henry smiled and patted Carter on the shoulder. "I need to go," he said abruptly, getting off his barstool. "Thanks again for your help tonight, Carter." He reached into his pocket and placed a shiny metal ball on the bar in front of him. It took a moment for Carter to recognize it as a jingle bell. With a wary eye on Henry, he picked it up, the bell tinkling slightly.

"If you ever need me, just give that a jingle," he said seriously. "It only works three times, so make sure it's really important, okay?"

Carter was confused, and wondered if he was drunker than he thought . . . or if Henry was some kind of lunatic. "What are you talking about?"

A huge grin split Henry's face. "I'm talking about second chances, Carter. An opportunity to set things right." He slapped the bar beside him to emphasize his words.

Carter stared at him blankly for a moment before erupting in laughter. The guy was obviously crazy. "Okay . . . right . . . yeah," he said, putting the bell in his pocket. "Thanks for the drink." He lifted his nearly empty glass in salute.

"Don't lose the bell, Carter," Henry warned, suddenly solemn. "If you do, there won't be any way for me to help you."

Carter stared at him for a moment, his smile falling as a slight shiver raced up his spine. "Who are you?"

Henry smiled softly, turning for the door. "Go home and go to bed, Carter," he suggested. "There's a cab outside. It'll all make more sense in the morning." He walked out, the door drifting shut silently behind him.

Carter stared after him for a moment, then turned back to the TV, finishing his drink as he watched a little more of the movie. He set the glass on the counter, along with a five dollar tip, and headed outside. Sure enough, there was a cab waiting at the curb. Carter got inside and slumped against the seat, tugging his tie loose as the driver pulled away from the bar.

The drive back to the hotel was quick and filled with flashes of Kenzie—memories of their time together . . . laughter and tears . . . always interspersed with the new, troubling images of her with the tall, dark man.

Kenzie . . .

If only . . .

"Hey, buddy, is this the place?" The cab driver's voice jarred him out of his thoughts.

Carter looked out the window at his hotel and nodded at the driver, handing him a twenty before getting out. He took a deep breath, focusing on walking a straight line through the lobby and into the elevator, giving in to his inebriation and leaning against the wall once the doors shut. He managed to make it down the hall and to his room, getting the door open after three attempts. He shrugged out of his jacket as the door closed, toeing off his shoes before falling into bed, fully dressed. He felt a digging in his hip and reached into his pocket, pulling out the little bell with an irritated moan.

He fell asleep with it clutched in his hand, finally succumbing to the oblivion of a dark, dreamless sleep.

CHAPTER THREE

rockin' around the christmas tree

A loud whirring sound pounded its way into Carter's brain. He moaned, pulling the pillow over his head and wishing whoever was stabbing ice picks into his eye sockets would please stop.

Immediately.

The whirring paused, only to start up again and Carter rolled over, giving up on any hope of sleeping off his hangover. Maybe there was construction going on outside the hotel . . . or someone had ridden a Harley into his suite. At any rate, sleep was apparently off the table.

He frowned at the feel of rough fabric under his cheek. He'd thought he made it to the bed last night, but maybe he'd fallen asleep on the floor. Without opening his eyes, he reached out to touch whatever he was sleeping on.

Huh. A couch.

But he thought the couch in his suite was leather . . . white leather, if he recalled correctly.

Fighting the pain throbbing in his skull, Carter opened his bleary eyes slowly, blinking them to focus on his surroundings. He stared unseeingly for a moment, unable to rationalize the vision before him.

He wasn't in his hotel room. He was in a house . . . in a living room. He scanned the room slowly, taking in the overfilled bookshelf . . . the large-screen TV in the corner partially blocked by the Christmas tree . . . the two matching arm chairs positioned across a low coffee table from the couch where he was lying.

Where in the world was he?

"Morning," a raspy voice said on a yawn as the owner of the voice walked across the room in front of him toward the kitchen. "I made some coffee if you want some."

Carter sat up slowly, squinting at the man talking to him. He wore loose pajama pants and a ratty t-shirt, but he was familiar—the olive skin and short-cropped black hair pinging a memory. "Noah?"

He hadn't seen Noah Collins since he left Seattle . . . barely spoken to him since then. And he was in his living room?

"What are you doing here?" Carter asked in shock.

Noah laughed, taking a sip of his coffee as he leaned against the kitchen counter. "It's my house, jerk. How much did you have to drink last night, anyway?"

Before Carter could answer, a bouncing blur swept through the room toward Noah.

22

"Merry Christmas, handsome," the blur said once she'd stilled, planting a kiss on Noah's waiting lips.

"Lydia?" Carter said, finally realizing he must be in some crazy dream. A dream where his former best friend and his sister were apparently involved. And he slept on their couch.

Lydia ignored him, easily jumping into Noah's arms and wrapping her long legs around his waist. Noah caught her with one arm, not even spilling his coffee, and returned her increasingly passionate kisses.

"Ugh. I don't need to see that," Carter complained, clenching his eyes shut at the sight of his sister, dressed only in a t-shirt and underwear, mauling a guy right in front of him.

Without missing a beat, Lydia said over her shoulder. "Then go home, Carter. That's where you should be anyway. It's Christmas." She slid down Noah's body, kissing him once more before turning to her brother as she tugged her long blond hair into a bun, securing it with a band from around her wrist. "Did you even call Kenzie last night and let her know where you were?"

Carter blinked at her. "Kenzie?"

Lydia rolled her eyes. "You didn't, did you? Well, lucky for you, *I* did. Otherwise, she would have the police out looking for you. You should be grateful we even let you in last night after Kenzie tossed you out."

Carter's head was swimming. "She tossed me out?"

23

Lydia leaned in, sniffing him slightly. "Ugh. You smell like a brewery. You really don't remember last night?" At Carter's blank look, she continued. "The Christmas party? Getting drunk as a skunk and going home? Kenzie telling you to get your act together or not bother coming back?" Lydia shook her head in a mix of pity and frustration. "Seriously, Carter, when are you going to get it through that thick head of yours that Kenzie's the best thing that ever happened to you?"

Carter couldn't argue that point. "I know," he said quietly.

"Well then act like it!" she exclaimed, slapping him on the back of the head and causing the relentless pounding to intensify. He heard Noah chuckle.

"Go home, Carter," Lydia said on a sigh. "We'll see you back here at six for dinner, right?"

Carter hesitated, but decided that in a dream it was usually best to play along. "Six. Right."

"Okay." Lydia leaned in and kissed his cheek. "And take a shower, for God's sake."

The next thing he knew, he'd been all but shoved out the door. He turned to the long gravel driveway, huddled in his jacket, and wondered what to do next. Then he was hit by something strange.

No snow.

It had been snowing the night before. Snowing hard. But in the gray light of dawn, a light drizzle fell from the sky and water dripped from the eaves on the house and the trees around him. Carter pulled his hand from his coat pocket, finally realizing he was holding something. Uncurling his fingers, he recognized the little bell that Henry had given him the night before.

Shoving it into his pants pocket, he also noticed he was not wearing the clothes he'd gone to sleep in. Instead, he was dressed in a pair of dark jeans and boots, a blue button-down over a white thermal, and a heavy denim jacket. He rubbed a hand over his face, surprised to find it mostly covered by hair. He'd never had a beard before. His job had always required him to remain clean-shaven, except for the occasional rugged five-o-clock shadow when he was embedded in a war zone or something.

What a weird dream. Lydia and Noah were together. He and Kenzie were apparently together, although having some issues. And evidently, he was some kind of lumberjack.

Carter sighed and stepped off the front porch and walked down the little path to the driveway where two small cars and an SUV were parked. He turned back to the little A-frame, trying to determine if he recognized it.

He didn't.

He looked down the driveway toward the street, wondering where he was supposed to go. On a hunch, he searched his pockets, letting out a victorious chuckle when he found a cell phone and a set of keys. He pressed the button on a key fob and was rewarded by the sound of a door unlocking. He approached the little sedan parked next to the SUV and opened the driver's side door.

Carter looked over the little black car. It was a Honda Civic . . . late 90s, he guessed, with a creased rear quarter panel streaked with a bit of yellow paint. He wondered what he'd hit. With a heavy sigh he folded his tall frame into the driver's seat and tapped his fingers on the steering wheel, again wondering what to do next.

Where to go?

Normally, in a dream, it was pretty obvious what to do. Actually, now that he thought about it, normally things just kind of happened around you and you went along for the ride. The quiet around him was strange. There was nobody else around, and the only sound was the dripping rain and his own breathing. Once again he looked around, still unsure of where he was.

It sure didn't look like New York.

Smoke curled from the chimney of Noah's little house, twisting through the towering pines and cedars to the gray skies overhead. No, it didn't look like New York at all. It almost looked like . . .

Carter reached into his back pocket and pulled out a worn leather wallet. He flipped it open, absently noting a handful of credit cards and about twenty bucks in cash. He examined the driver's license behind a sheet of clear plastic, his bearded face staring back at him, unsmiling. He looked at the address.

Woodlawn.

Woodlawn, Washington. His hometown . . . a town he hadn't been back to but a handful of times since he'd left for New York.

Carter could only assume that seeing Kenzie the night before had sparked the rather strange dream he was having. He found himself unwilling to wake up, however. At least, not until he'd seen Kenzie.

He concentrated, wondering if he could make it that far. Usually, it wasn't long after you realized you were dreaming that you were already half-awake. Studying the address on his driver's license, he decided he might as well try.

He started the little car, or at least tried to. It took three attempts before the engine finally caught and he pulled out of the driveway. Once he made it to the main road, things started to look familiar. He realized that Noah had built his house on a piece of land they all used to hang out on when they were in high school. If Carter recalled correctly, there was a swimming hole about a hundred feet beyond Noah's house. They'd had a lot of fun at that pond over the years.

It *had* been fun growing up in Woodlawn. Established as a logging town, Woodlawn had prospered until the early nineties when the endangered Spotted Owl forced the end of logging in old growth forests in the northwest. Some said it was only a matter of time, anyway—the loss of those forests would have come sooner or later—but it was a blow to the little town. The mills shut down, jobs were lost, families moved away. But those that stayed became a tight-knit group. And Woodlawn had survived, transforming into a tourist stop for those heading to the Washington coast with its cafes, antique shops, and quaint bed and breakfasts.

Carter found himself smiling as he made his way through town. It hadn't changed much, not that he'd expected it would. It made sense that it would look as he remembered it. He turned down Calawah Way, past the mobile home park, then up Trillium Avenue and onto Mayberry Street, searching the houses for the right number.

He pulled up in front of a white two-story house, with blue trim and a black door. A Big Wheel lay overturned in the driveway next to a gray mini-van, and the front lawn was thick, evidencing the weeks of rainy weather. Carter climbed out of the car, surprised to find his stomach in knots.

It's only a dream. He said it to himself over and over, like a mantra. Still, he was inexplicably nervous.

He fiddled with the keys in his hand, wondering if he should knock or just walk in. He ended up not having to decide, however, because just as he stepped up onto the front porch, the door was thrown open and he was hit in the chest with a heavy duffle bag.

Carter staggered slightly, catching the bag before it landed on the wet ground. Before he could fully recover, another smaller bag hit him in the head.

"What the—" He stumbled back off the porch and lost his balance, landing on his butt with a grunt as another bag slammed into his stomach. He looked up into a familiar face glaring down at him like an avenging angel.

"Violet?" Carter's voice cracked in surprise at the appearance of Noah's younger sister. "What the hell is going on?"

"What's going on?" she hissed. "Seriously, Carter, do you even have to ask? Kenzie called me last night in tears after what you pulled and you expected to come back here and all would be forgiven? Not this time. No way!"

Carter managed to get to his feet. "Where's Kenzie?"

She crossed her arms over her chest and blew a strand of black hair away from her cheek. "She doesn't want to see you."

A chill ran over his skin at the thought. "Violet. I want to talk to her."

"Too bad," she retorted. "She had a feeling you'd stop by and I was more than happy to stick around to make sure you got your stuff." She waved a hand at the bags. "Feel free to take it over to Noah's or wherever you're staying, because she doesn't want you here."

"Vi, it's Christmas." It was lame, but the only argument he could think of. He really had no idea what was going on, after all . . . and, dream or no dream, he wanted to see Kenzie.

Violet Collins was not one to succumb to pity, however. "You should have thought of that before you took off—*on Christmas Eve, Carter*—and acted like a drunken moron. You know it's not just about last night. She's tired of it all, Carter. She's tired of you."

With that, Violet walked back into the house and slammed the door, leaving Carter standing stunned at the bottom of the porch stairs.

A sickening feeling twisted in his stomach as he realized a few things. First, he hurt. His butt was sore and his hand was bleeding where he scraped it on the walkway trying to catch his fall. Second, the rain was falling harder and he was starting to shiver, his clothes cold and wet and his hair dripping into his eyes.

Which led him to a conclusion that was illogical . . . impossible . . . but twitching at the edge of his consciousness. One he didn't even want to consider.

Carter closed his eyes, willing himself to awaken. He'd done it hundreds of times in the past when a nightmare got too frightening. All he had to do was concentrate and he'd open his eyes and be back in his own bed, this bizarre experience melting away into barely recognizable glimpses.

Just a few more minutes.

He waited.

The rain fell harder, thunder clapped, and he saw lightning flash through his closed eyelids.

Little while longer.

Any time now.

"Carter?" A quiet voice forced his eyes open. He inhaled sharply as her face came into view.

Kenzie. Her dark hair and warm, brown eyes. Her turned up nose and soft, pink lips. Lips turned down a little at the edges, tight with tension.

"Why are you standing in the rain?" she asked, her arms clutched across her stomach defensively as she stood in the open doorway. "I thought you left."

Carter stared at her in silence for a moment, unable to find words. She was dressed in a pair of faded jeans and t-shirt under a red plaid flannel shirt with the arms rolled up. He wondered if it was one of his.

He found he liked that idea.

She took in the wet bags lying on the ground and Carter's soaked clothes and sighed. "I'm sorry about Vi," she said finally. "You know how protective she is, and after last night . . ." Her voice drifted off as she looked away, brushing at her cheeks. Carter's heart sank as he realized she was crying.

"Kenzie . . . I'm sorry."

She shrugged, looking into the distance again. "I know, Carter. You're always sorry. That's the problem, isn't it?" She stepped back from the door. "You might as well come in and get dried off. We can talk about this later. I know the kids would love to see you."

Carter's step faltered as he moved forward.

Wait a second. What?

Kids?

Chapter

FOUR

tiny tots with their eyes all aglow

Carter swallowed thickly as he scooped up the bags and walked into the house. He noticed that Kenzie stepped back as he approached, obviously not wanting to touch him. Carter hesitated in the entryway, unsure of where to go.

"Go upstairs and get a shower," Kenzie told him quietly. "The kids fell asleep in the other room, so you have a little time." She looked at him sadly for a moment, before walking away and into what he could see was a kitchen in the back of the house. Violet was leaning against the counter glaring at him, and he turned away quickly to climb the stairs.

He walked down the hallway, peeking into each room as he passed it. The first one was painted pale blue with clouds across the ceiling and a low bed with a dark blue quilt in the corner. A few toy cars were scattered across a colorful rug in the middle of the floor and a huge stuffed panda huddled under a window on the other side of the room. The next was obviously a little girl's room, featuring pale pink and yellow-striped walls and a white bed with a mound of stuffed animals covering the pillows. A small Jack-and-Jill bathroom stood between the two rooms, painted a brighter yellow, with multicolored towels and tropical fish accents.

Across the hall he found the master bedroom, decorated in pale sand and dark brown, with accents of deep red. Carter slipped off his shoes and padded quietly into the room, taking in the homey feel. The furniture was aged wood, gleaming and obviously polished regularly. He reached out to touch the huge pile of pillows on the bed, his fingers trailing over the country-style quilt in shades of red and brown. It wasn't his taste, typically, but something about the room, and the bed, made him feel comfortable. He smiled at a picture of him and Kenzie on one of the bedside tables, Kenzie laughing as he nuzzled her neck. The obvious joy in the photograph filled him with a pang of longing. Next to it was a picture of two small children—a little boy holding a baby girl in his arms and grinning widely. Carter found himself grinning in response, the boy's warm brown eyes and toothy smile a mirror image of Kenzie's.

Carter shivered, and decided he needed to get out of his wet clothes. He was cold.

He was *cold.* The impossible thought he'd been trying not to think reared its ugly head yet again. How could he be cold?

Shaking it off, Carter stripped off his wet clothes and winced as the fabric brushed against his scraped hand. He gathered up the soggy mess, took it into the bathroom, and set it on the counter as he started the shower. Ducking his head under the hot water, he let the warmth seep into his chilled bones and tried to relax, again willing himself to wake up. There was no sense sticking around in the dream if Kenzie was so angry at him, after all. Carter breathed deeply, inhaling the scent of the coconut body wash and shampoo he'd found in the shower. He thought about shaving off the unfamiliar beard, then decided it against it, not wanting to take the time.

When the water ran cold, he gave up on waking up, the sense of foreboding inching through his now warm body. He dried off, and dug in the bags for some dry clothes, settling on another flannel shirt and jeans. Running a hand through his still-damp hair, he emerged from the bedroom and walked tentatively down the steps in search of Kenzie.

He found her curled up on a worn brown couch next to a brightly-lit Christmas tree and the remnants of a wild Christmas morning. Fortunately, Violet the guard dog was nowhere to be found. Toys and shredded gift wrap littered the floor and Carter stood in the doorway, nervously tucking his hands in his jean pockets. Kenzie's sad eyes turned toward him just as a pile of paper on the floor shot up in all directions.

"Daddy!" a little boy plowed through the mess and wrapped himself around Carter's leg. "Where were you? You missed Christmas!" A gap in the boy's front teeth colored his words with a slight lisp, so it took Carter a moment to interpret what he'd said. He patted the boy awkwardly on the back.

"Uh, yeah, sorry about that," he said. "I, uh, had to go see . . . Aunt Lydia?" Carter glommed on to the first excuse he could think of.

"Auntie Lyd?" the boy repeated. An excited grin split his face, then just as quickly morphed into a pout. "How come you didn't take me?" He released Carter's leg, crossing his arms over his chest with a huff.

"Uh . . ." Carter's eyes flew to Kenzie, but she only raised an eyebrow in response. Carter lowered to a knee and reached tentatively toward the little boy. "I'm sorry . . . buddy. But you had to be here to see what Santa brought, right?"

The boy's face lit up. "I got a fire truck!" he exclaimed, his irritation instantly forgotten. "And a new bike!" He swept through the crumpled paper to where a shiny two-wheeler stood beneath the tree. "Mommy said I had to wait until it stopped raining to ride it, though. Is it still raining?" He rushed to the window and peered out. "It's just a little." He turned to Kenzie. "It's just a little raining, Mommy. Can I ride my bike now?"

Kenzie's lips quirked. "You have to get dressed first," she pointed out, "and wear your helmet."

The boy crossed his arms again in what Carter was quickly learning was a familiar gesture. "I don't wanna wear my helmet!"

"Brady, we've talked about this," Kenzie said in that warning voice common to moms around the world.

"Mo—omm! It makes my head itch!" he whined.

At that moment, a muffled whine came from the other corner of the room. Carter turned and saw a little pile of pillows and blankets near the end of the couch.

"Carter, could you help me out here, please?" Kenzie moved past him to the blanket pile, and lifted a little blond-haired girl to her shoulder, patting her back gently. Carter turned to face Brady, whose temper tantrum was escalating to epic proportions. His red face scrunched up as he inhaled deeply and Carter was sure he was about to let out a piercing scream.

At that moment, the little girl Kenzie was holding began to whimper a little, awakening to the tension around her. "Mommy, I'm hungry."

Kenzie murmured to her before turning back to her son. "Brady. No helmet. No bike," she said firmly, and the scream Carter dreaded filled the room.

"Carter?" Kenzie turned to him in annoyance.

"Daaadddyyy!" Brady cried, collapsing on the floor in heaving sobs.

"I'm hungry!" The little girl started to kick her feet, her whines gaining volume as Carter's stunned gaze took in the scene around him. The faces turned to him in expectation, waiting for him to deal with the situation . . . for him to be Dad.

It was too much. Carter felt his heart rate accelerate as his palms grew sweaty and his head swam. He began to back out of the room, away from the insanity.

It wasn't real.

It wasn't real.

But somehow, way deep down inside, Carter knew he was wrong. Somehow . . . somehow it *was* real. And with that thought, he panicked and did the only thing he could think of.

He ran.

He headed for the front door, but remembered something that Henry had said to him the night before. He couldn't get past the feeling that the strange man had something to do with all of this, and if he was right, and this *was* real, Henry was the only one who could help him. He turned and ran up the stairs to the master bedroom, the cries and screams in the other room fading slightly as he made it to the second floor.

Carter stumbled into the bathroom, grabbing his pile of wet clothes and searching the pockets.

"Where is it?" he mumbled to himself, just before his hands closed on the little metal bell. He pulled it out of his pocket gingerly, his eyes narrowed on it in suspicion. It looked like a normal jingle bell—the kind you'd see everywhere at this time of year. Carefully, he grasped it by the tiny loop on the top and shook it, the tinkle echoing off the shower tiles. Without realizing it, he'd clenched his eyes shut as he rang the bell, and he slowly opened them, waiting for whatever was supposed to happen.

Nothing.

Carter stood and threw the bell onto the counter. "Figures," he mumbled as he stomped back into the bedroom. He came to an abrupt halt at the sight of Henry standing next to the bed.

"Hello, Carter."

"You!" Carter growled, taking a step toward him and tightening his fists in an effort to control himself. "What have you done to me?"

"Only what you asked for," Henry said brightly as he plopped onto the edge of the bed and hugged a pillow to his chest.

"What . . . did you drug me or something?" Carter asked. "Hypnotize me?" He thought for a moment. "You put something in my drink last night, didn't you?"

Henry laughed and stretched out on his side, propping his head on his hand. "No, Carter. Nothing like that. You asked for this. Don't you remember? The one thing in your past you'd change if you could—you wouldn't have chickened out ten years ago and you would have asked Kenzie to marry you."

"I—" He blinked in confusion. "I never told you that. How did you know that?"

Henry smiled. "I have an unusual . . . insight into people," he said, waving his hand with a flourish. "Well, Carter, you got your wish. You proposed on Christmas Eve and you got married six months later. You have two children, a house, two cars . . . the American dream."

Carter glared at him. "This isn't real."

"It's as real as you want it to be."

"It's a dream."

"You know it's not, Carter."

Carter was silent for a moment, then said quietly, "Kenzie hates me."

Henry shrugged. "Nobody's perfect."

Carter rolled his eyes. "I don't want this. I mean . . . I want Kenzie, but not like this. We're supposed to be *happy*."

Henry got up off the bed. "It was one choice . . . one *change* . . . and this is the result," he said. "You wanted to correct the mistake of not asking Kenzie to marry you ten years ago and you have. What you do now is up to you." Henry tilted his head as if listening to something. "I've gotta run," he said.

"No, wait," Carter exclaimed. "You have to get me out of here."

"No can do, Carter," Henry said with a grin, straightening his pristine white sweater. "You asked for this, now you've got to see it through." He moved toward the window.

"You mean I'm stuck here *forever?*" Carter exclaimed as panicked frustration swept through him. "What about my job? I'm supposed to start my new segment next week! And what the hell are we doing in Woodlawn? What about Kenzie's books?"

"Keep track of the bell, Carter. Only use it for emergencies. You only have two left," Henry warned.

A little voice drew Carter's attention to the doorway. "Daddy?" Brady hiccupped slightly, his face still red with the remnants of his tantrum. "Who are you talking to?"

Carter turned back to the window, but Henry was gone. "What the—" he murmured, hurrying to the window and pushing it open. He stuck his head out, but there was no sign that anyone had been there.

"Daddy?" Brady walked toward him, the feet of his pajamas flopping on the carpet. "I'm sorry I made you mad." His downcast eyes tore at Carter's heart and he found himself falling to his knees in front of the little boy.

"It's okay, Brady," he said gently, lifting a hand to rub his son's head. "I'm not mad at you. I just . . . got a little scared, you know?"

Brady looked up in confusion. "Scared 'a what? You're a daddy. You're not supposed to be scared of anything." His lisp became more prominent with all of the S's in his sentence and it made Carter smile.

"Oh, daddies get scared too, sometimes," he said. "So, are you feeling better?" To his surprise, Brady reached up to him, forcing Carter to sit on the floor so he could climb into his lap.

"Yeah. I'm okay," he said, sniffling slightly. "Mommy said I needed to have a time out."

Carter smirked. "Are you supposed to be in your room right now?"

Brady shrugged, not meeting his gaze.

"I'll tell you what," Carter said conspiratorially. "I won't say anything if you promise to wear your helmet when you ride your new bike."

Brady sighed heavily. "Okay," he agreed, drawing out the word so Carter knew it was a huge concession.

Seeing the opportunity to find out a little about the world he now found himself in, Carter decided to prod the child for some information.

"Say, Brady, you want to play a game?"

Brady looked up, his face brightening. "What kind of game?"

"Umm . . . it's kind of a pretend game."

"Like Aliens and Space Rangers?" It took Carter a moment to decipher "*Alienth and Thpace Rangerth.*"

He laughed. "Kind of. I'll give you clues and you have to guess the answer."

"Okay."

"Ready?"

"Yes, Daddy."

Carter pretended to think really hard. "Okay . . . she's a little girl and lives in our house."

Brady shook his head pityingly. "That's too easy. It's my sister."

"You have to say her name."

"Peyton." Brady rolled his eyes, already tiring of the game.

"Peyton," Carter repeated quietly, wondering how he and Kenzie had decided on that name. Brady was easy—it was a family name. But Peyton? He couldn't think of a connection to that name. Not that he didn't like it, because he did.

"Daddy? Are we still playing?" Brady toyed with the zipper on his pajamas, obviously getting bored.

"Okay," Carter said with a smile. "This is the place where I work."

"Umm . . ." Brady's eyes scrunched up as he thought. "It's the paper place."

"The paper place?" Carter considered that for a moment. "You mean I work at a paper?"

Brady nodded. "The paper place."

Carter was relieved he was still a journalist of some sort, but wondered which newspaper he worked at. It seemed a long commute to work for the Seattle Times, but he supposed he could be some sort of columnist.

"What about Mommy?" he asked.

"What about Mommy?" Brady repeated, his brow creased in confusion.

"Where does Mommy work?"

Brady rolled his eyes. "Mommy works at my school."

"Your school? Doing what?"

"Daddy, I don't like this game," Brady said in reply. "It's not fun at all. Can we play Old Maid instead?"

Carter smiled at the boy. It was difficult not to be enchanted by him. He was like a miniature Kenzie with his dark hair and eyes, turned-up nose, and quick smile. Carter could tell that he was smart as well . . . also something he credited to Kenzie.

Carter made a show of looking toward the window. "Old Maid?" he said. "I was thinking since it's stopped raining we'd take that bike for a spin."

"Yay!" Brady squealed, jumping to his feet and running into the hall. "I'll get my helmet!"

CHAPTER FIVE

i'll be home for christmas

"Okay, remember I'm right here."

"I know, Daddy."

"Don't be scared."

"I'm not."

"Okay, push off and go, buddy."

Brady grunted as he pushed the pedal down, his bike wobbling as he began to roll down the sidewalk. "Daddy!"

"It's okay," Carter encouraged him, his hands on either side of the bike seat—not touching, but close enough to grab it if he started to fall. "You're doing great! Keep pedaling!"

The wobbling lessened as Brady sped up. "I'm doing it!"

"Keep going!"

Brady raced down the sidewalk and Carter began to run to try and keep up with him. "You got this, buddy!"

Brady pulled away, pumping wildly, the bike rolling steady for a long, happy moment.

Then . . .

"Daddy!" he yelled in a worried voice, just before the bike tipped over and he fell onto the hard concrete.

"Brady!" Carter ran up to him and dropped to his knees to pull the bike off the little boy as his stomach clenched in fear. "Are you okay?"

To his surprise, Brady jumped to his feet. "Did you see? I did it! I went so fast!" He bounced up and down. "I want to go again."

Carter laughed and turned the bike around. "Okay. Next time, just remember you have to put your foot down when you stop."

He took off again confidently, the bike moving smoothly down the sidewalk as Carter ran alongside him. This time, when he reached their front yard, he hit the brakes and put his foot down on the ground with a huge grin on his face.

Caught up in the moment, Carter swept the little boy up into his arms, spinning him around as the bike clattered forgotten to the sidewalk. Brady squealed and Carter couldn't hold back his laugh.

"Daddy, I'm dizzy," Brady shrieked.

Carter gently placed his son back on his feet, not releasing him until he regained his balance. Over Brady's shoulder he caught a flash of movement in the living room window. Kenzie was standing there, rocking Peyton on her hip with a soft smile on her face as she watched them. The smile fell a bit when she met Carter's eyes.

Right then Carter made a decision. Dream or not, he was going to make things right with Kenzie.

Because—dream or not—he was still in love with her.

The rest of the morning passed peacefully, if not comfortably. Kenzie avoided talking to him— even being in the same room with him—but had yet to ask him to leave.

Carter took that as a good sign.

At Brady's insistence, Carter opened his Christmas gifts. More flannel from Kenzie—big surprise. Carter wondered when he'd become so fond of dressing like a grunge rocker from the nineties. He smiled and thanked her, though, and was suitably impressed by the little wooden tool box Brady had painted blue and yellow for him.

Once the gifts were opened, Kenzie put Peyton down for a nap and sent Brady to take his new toys to his room. Carter sat awkwardly for a moment, then stood to start picking up the torn gift wrap and bows off the floor. He crumpled a wad into a tight ball, and was wondering what to do with it when Kenzie appeared with a huge garbage bag.

"Here." She held it out to him and he deposited his bundle inside before taking it from her.

They worked in silence for a while, clearing the aftermath of Hurricane Brady, when Carter heard Kenzie release a heavy sigh. Carter watched her out of the corner of his eye. She looked tired and worn, and—God help him—so incredibly beautiful.

"This doesn't fix anything," she finally said quietly. "I don't want to ruin Christmas for Brady, so we'll go to dinner at Noah and Lydia's and spend time with our families, but tomorrow, we need to settle a few things."

"Okay."

"I mean it, Carter," she said firmly. "I'm not going to just give in this time. Something needs to change, or . . ."

Carter swallowed thickly. "Or . . ." he finally prodded, afraid of the answer.

"Or we're through." Her words were quiet, barely a whisper, but they cut through Carter's heart.

"I'll do whatever it takes," he told her.

"I've heard that before."

"But I really mean it this time."

Kenzie laughed humorlessly. "I've heard that before, too."

Carter thrust the last of the paper into the garbage bag, tying it tightly and letting it drop to the floor as he ran a hand through his hair. "I don't know what to say, Kenzie. I don't want to lose you."

Before I even had you, he added silently.

"Carter you haven't had me—we haven't had *each other*—for a long time," she said, her eyes wide and sad. "I don't know. Maybe it's time to let it go."

"That's not what I want."

Kenzie pursed her lips. "It's not all about you, Carter."

"Mommy?" Brady appeared at the doorway, rubbing his eyes. "I'm hungry."

Without meeting Carter's gaze again, Kenzie moved toward her son. "How about a sandwich?" she suggested. "Then I think it's time for a rest before we go to Auntie Lydia's."

"But I'm not tired!"

"Brady," Kenzie's warning tone made Carter smile as the two made their way to the kitchen, their voices still carrying to him through the quiet house.

"Okay," Brady agreed grumpily, "but can I have peanut butter and jelly?"

"Okay."

The tension continued through the afternoon, although—true to her word—Kenzie didn't bring up their problems again and instead put on a smiling face. While Brady and Peyton napped, she cleaned the kitchen, although Carter thought it was more out of a desire to avoid him than anything else. The kitchen was spotless.

Carter took the opportunity to roam the house, flipping through photo albums and peeking into drawers. He knew that it was technically his house, but he still felt like he was snooping uninvited. What he found seemed to pose more questions than answers, however. He found his college diploma, as well as Kenzie's, but no sign of her Master's degree. And when he came across a shelf in their apparently shared office covered with "World's Greatest Teacher" mugs and miniature trophies, he realized Kenzie must have become a teacher instead of an author.

He wondered what led to that decision.

He also wondered how he ended up working at the *Woodlawn Weekly*, a newspaper he'd never heard of. He came across a stack of the papers, as well as some business cards in a desk drawer. Evidently he was Editor-in-Chief.

"We need to be at Lydia's in an hour," Kenzie said from the office doorway. Carter jumped, immediately flushing with guilt, but quelled his panic when he realized Kenzie was not surprised or irritated by his presence in the room. It was his office, after all.

"Okay."

"I'll get the kids up and ready, and if you could keep them entertained while I shower?" she asked tentatively, as if she was used to him protesting such a request.

Carter shrugged. "Of course."

"I ironed your blue shirt. It's on the bed if you want to change."

Carter blinked, unused to having such things done for him. "Thanks," he said finally. "I appreciate it."

Kenzie nodded slightly in acknowledgement and left.

Carter made his way to the bedroom and dressed quickly before heading down the hall toward Brady's room. He fought a chuckle at the sight that greeted him. A very excited Brady was jumping on the bed while Kenzie tried to pull a striped sweater over his head.

"Daddy!" he exclaimed when he spotted Carter in the doorway. "We're going to Auntie Lyd's!"

Carter grinned. "I know, buddy. But we can't go if you don't let Mommy help you get dressed."

"But I'm so 'cited! My body doesn't want to stop jumpin'!" he argued, punctuating every word with another jump on the squeaking mattress.

Carter walked into the room and scooped up the giggling boy before he sat on the bed, plopping Brady down on his lap. "Just try for a second," Carter said. "We'll count to five and I'll bet Mommy's done. One . . ."

Brady smiled at the game. "Two . . ."

Kenzie pulled the sweater over Brady's head. "Three . . ."

One arm through, then the other. "Four . . ."

Kenzie yanked a pair of shoes onto Brady's feet, working quickly to tie them. "Four and a half . . ." Carter said, drawing the words out slowly.

Kenzie finished tying the shoes, and kissed Brady's cheek with a loud smack. "Five!"

"Done!" Brady wiggled from Carter's lap and ran from the room. "Time to go!"

Kenzie sat back on her heels, pushing her hair out of her face. "Thanks," she said. "Could you get Peyton? She's in her room, ready to go. I'm just going to grab a quick shower."

Carter felt a stab of apprehension at the thought of caring for Peyton. He had very little experience with children in general, let alone little girls. But he hid his fear and smiled instead. "Sure. No problem."

"I'll be ready in twenty," Kenzie said, looking away abruptly and walking down the hall to their bedroom.

Carter approached Peyton's room slowly, trying not to panic as the pink and yellow stripes surrounded him with the unfamiliar essence of femininity. The little girl sat in the middle of the floor, cradling a baby doll and cooing quietly. Carter took a moment to study her. In the shadow of Brady's enthusiasm, he hadn't really had an opportunity to do so until that moment.

Her blond hair was a wild mess on her head, the nearly-white strands shimmering in the subtle lamplight. Carter smiled ruefully at the knowledge that she'd probably fight the cowlicks for the rest of her life, and hoped she wouldn't curse her father for the genes that condemned her to such a fate. He had been tow-headed as well, when he was a child. His hair started to darken when he hit puberty and by the time he was an adult, it was barely light enough to still be called blond.

Carter smiled softly as Peyton sang to the doll, a tuneless melody with words he couldn't decipher. Eventually, she realized she was being watched, and her gaze lifted to meet Carter's.

"Hi, Daddy," she whispered quietly, evidently trying not to wake the baby.

It was a moment before Carter could reply, because when her big eyes met his, he lost his breath. It was like looking into a mirror. The luminous hazel eyes with flecks of green and gold staring back at him were his own. It was unsettling . . . overwhelming . . . yet, at the same time, he was filled with a pride and possessiveness that nearly knocked him over.

His child. *His daughter.*

Was it possible to fall in love with someone so quickly?

He stepped toward her tentatively, dropping into a crouch on the rug. "Hi, Peyton." Unable to resist, he reached out to touch a wayward strand of her hair. "What are you doing?"

"Taking care of Baby. She's sleepy," she whispered.

"Is she coming to Aunt Lydia's with us?"

Peyton nodded solemnly. "'Course. She always comes with me."

Carter smiled. "Well, can we go downstairs? As soon as Mommy's ready, we need to get going."

"'Kay, Daddy." She patted his cheek, scratching his beard softly, before handing him the doll unceremoniously as she got to her feet. Carter held it awkwardly by one arm.

"Daddy!" she chided. "You have to hold her gently!" She reached out to wrap his arms around the plastic doll.

"Is that right?" Carter asked, still a little awed by the pretty child. He adjusted his hold. "Is that better?"

Peyton nodded, taking Carter's pant leg and tugging him from the room. "Do you think Auntie Lyd will have cookies?"

"Umm . . . maybe."

"Peanut butter? They're my favorite."

"Mine, too!"

Peyton looked at him suspiciously. "I know that, Daddy."

Carter grinned. "Of course you do."

They walked downstairs, only to find Brady running wildly from one room to another, his arms spread wide as he made airplane noises.

"I'm gonna fly to Auntie Lyd's!" he yelled from the kitchen.

"Maybe we should take the car instead," Carter suggested.

"Nope. Flying's faster."

"You can't fly, Brady," Peyton said, her tone much older than her little body as she propped her fists on her hips. "You don't have wings."

Brady came to stop in front of her. "Can so."

"Can not."

"Can so!"

"Can not!" she screamed.

"Whoa! Wait a second." Carter tried to intervene, scrambling for a way to defuse the situation. Two pairs of eyes turned to him, apparently waiting for him to declare a winner in the little standoff.

Carter had no idea what to do.

Fortunately, he was spared by Kenzie coming down the stairs, pulling on a long coat as she hurried into the room. "Time to go!" she said cheerfully, successfully diverting the children's attention. "Bundle up if you want to go to Auntie Lydia's."

Brady and Peyton cheered, slipping on their coats and waiting patiently as Kenzie zipped them up. Carter watched the scene with mixed emotions.

On the one hand, he felt overwhelmed, with a wife and two children all dependent on him—and from what he'd learned so far, he was failing them.

On the other, the domestic scene filled him with a sense of peace and longing. It was something he hadn't known he wanted, even in the times when he's mourned the loss of Kenzie in his life with a fervency he didn't know he possessed.

But he did . . . want it, that is.

He realized it as he followed Kenzie out to the minivan and watched her strap Peyton into her car seat. As Brady sang Jingle Bells at the top of his lungs. As the van backfired before the engine finally caught, and they slowly backed out of the driveway.

As he caught a glimpse of Kenzie—his *wife*—in the seat next to him.

He wanted this life. Even if it meant he never set foot on foreign soil or appeared on the national news. He *wanted* this life.

But his heart sank when he made another realization.

He may have wanted it, but he wasn't sure Kenzie did anymore.

chapter SIX

home for the holidays

T hey pulled up in front of Noah and Lydia's house and Carter helped Kenzie get the kids out of the van, and held Peyton's hand as they made their way to the front door. He noticed several cars in the driveway and wondered who else was going to be at dinner.

"Merry Christmas!" Lydia shouted as she threw open the front door, dropping to her knees to wrap Peyton and Brady into a tight hug. "How are my most favoritest niece and nephew in the whole wide world?" she asked, pulling back to kiss their cheeks.

Brady giggled. "Auntie Lyd, we're your only niece and nephew," he pointed out.

"Well, you're still my favorite," she said with another squeeze. She leaned in to stage whisper to Peyton. "Go on into the kitchen. There might be some peanut butter cookies waiting for you in there."

The children cheered and ran off toward the kitchen. Kenzie called out after them, "Only one until after dinner!" She turned to Lydia. "You spoil them, you know," she said, leaning in to hug her sister-in-law.

"Auntie's prerogative," Lydia retorted, turning to Carter. "You look better."

Carter smiled slightly. "Feel better."

Lydia took a step back from the door. "Well, come on in. Mom and Dad are here. And Stitch has already confiscated the remote," she added with a laugh.

Kenzie rolled her eyes. "Typical."

"Oh, cut the guy a little slack, Kenzie," Lydia replied, linking her elbow with Kenzie's. "It's the holidays. Let him have his fun."

Carter trailed behind them, closing the door quietly and shrugging out of his coat. He followed Kenzie's lead, hanging it in a closet off the living room before they converged on the kitchen. Noah was stirring something on the stove, a ruffled apron wrapped around his waist. Carter finally noticed that his friend wore a wedding band, as did Lydia. He wondered how long they'd been married.

"It smells wonderful in here," Kenzie said, crossing to kiss Noah on the cheek. "Anything I can do to help?"

He waved her off. "No, we've got it under control. Go and say hello to Mom and Dad. Violet's in there, too," he said, casting a warning glance toward Carter. "You might want to steer clear of her."

55

Carter grimaced. "Yeah, she's not too happy with me." He watched as Lydia and Kenzie headed toward the family room. "She almost didn't let me in the house this morning."

"Well, you can hardly blame her," Noah pointed out. "It's not the first time, Carter."

Carter sighed heavily at the reminder that he had a pattern of letting Kenzie down. "It's going to be the last," he said quietly.

Noah studied him for a moment. "You seem different," he observed. "I can't put my finger on it, but . . ." He shook his head, adjusting the heat on the stove. "Anyway, Vi brought her new boyfriend, so she'll be on her best behavior." He pulled a masher out of a drawer and starting in on a pot of potatoes.

"Boyfriend?" Carter repeated. "Who's the lucky guy?"

"Macon Bridges."

Carter choked slightly. "You're kidding."

Noah grinned. "Nope."

"But . . . she'll eat him alive!"

Noah laughed. "I thought so too, but the guy can actually hold his own. And Vi really likes him. It's sickening really . . . she's putty in his hands."

"Putty? Violet?" Carter scoffed.

Noah added some butter to the potatoes. "You'll have to see it for yourself." He dumped the mashed potatoes into a bowl and placed them in the oven to keep them warm. Carter eyed him carefully.

"Noah, can I ask you something?"

"Sure," he said distractedly.

"It's going to sound weird," Carter warned.

Noah's eyes crinkled as he smiled, wiping his hands on a towel as he turned to face his friend. "Shoot."

Carter took a deep breath. "Why didn't Kenzie finish grad school?"

Noah looked at him in confusion. "What?"

"Just humor me, okay?" Carter said in a rush. "Why didn't she finish?"

Noah replied slowly. "Well, you know, after you got laid off at the *Times*—"

"I got laid off?"

"What's this all about, Carter?"

"Please, Noah, just tell me."

Noah stared warily at Carter for a moment. "You were reporting at the *Seattle Times*. Kenzie had maybe a year left to get her Master's, but you got laid off . . . budget cuts."

"I never went to New York," Carter murmured, half to himself.

"No," Noah replied slowly, still confused by the strange conversation. "You turned down the internship before you and Kenzie got married."

He paused, but Carter nodded, motioning for him to continue.

"You decided to come back here to start your own weekly paper. Kenzie already had her teaching certificate because she was subbing to make ends meet. She got a job at Woodlawn Elementary and you started the *Weekly*."

"So she gave up writing?" Carter asked.

"Carter, you know this."

"Please, Noah . . . please."

Noah sighed, evidently worried his best friend had lost his mind. "She published a few short stories and magazine articles, but then she got pregnant with Brady, so she had to give it up," he told him. "Then Peyton came along, and you had to spend so much time at the paper . . . there just wasn't time for her to get back to it."

Carter's eyes drifted to the doorway as he heard Kenzie's laughter drift through. "Does she hate me for that?"

Noah laughed. "Kenzie doesn't hate you for anything, Carter."

"You could have fooled me."

"Kenzie *loves* you," Noah said emphatically, drawing Carter's attention back. "But a girl can only put up with so much."

"What have I done?" he asked. At first, Noah thought he was talking to himself, but Carter turned pleading eyes toward him. "Tell me, Noah. What did I do to her? Did I . . . Did I cheat on her?" He couldn't imagine doing such a thing, but given Kenzie's feelings, he had to ask the question.

Noah gaped at him for a moment. "What are you talking about?'

"Did I? I have to know what I'm up against here. Is there another woman?"

His friend stared at him for a long moment. "There are lots of ways to cheat, Carter," he pointed out. "Every time you put your job before your family. Every time you let your resentment about New York show. Every time you lashed out at her because life didn't go exactly the way you planned—"

Carter held up a hand. "I get the idea."

Noah turned off a burner and they stood in silence for a moment. "Are you going to tell me what this is all about?" he asked.

Carter rubbed his hands over his face. "I'm not exactly sure," he admitted. "I just know that I have to make things right. I . . . I need her, Noah."

"You got that right." He chuckled.

"So what do I do? How do I fix this?"

Noah smiled sadly at his friend. "I don't have any great words of wisdom, man," he said. "I'm afraid that's one you're going to have to figure out on your own."

Carter nodded. He was beginning to believe the very same thing.

"Here, take this," Noah said, handing Carter a bowl of rolls. "It's time to eat."

Carter helped Noah carry the food to the dining room table, but was distracted by a familiar voice in the other room. He set down the bowl and walked into the family room.

"Carter!" His mother, Claire, crossed the room, enveloping him in a tight hug. "Merry Christmas!"

To Carter's surprise, he had to swallow a lump in his throat. How long had it been since he'd hugged his mother? A year? It was before the assignment in Afghanistan. God, that was almost two years ago.

"Merry Christmas, Mom," he finally managed to get out before turning to hug his father. He smiled at the familiar scent of pipe smoke and his father's aftershave. "Good to see you, Dad."

"You too, son." David Reed pulled back to pat his shoulder. "How's everything at the paper?"

"Umm . . . good . . . good, I think," Carter stammered.

"I saw the exposé on the local nursing home," he said with a proud smile. "That was some solid work."

A non-committal grunt came from the leather recliner in front of the television. Carter gulped. Sheriff Jeremiah "Stitch" Monroe, so named because he once sewed up his own gunshot wound (although whether or not that was actually true, Carter never had the courage to ask), sat in the recliner, eyes focused on an old black and white movie. Besides being the most intimidating man Carter had ever known, he was also Kenzie's father.

Carter cleared his throat. "Hello, Sheriff," he said with a nod toward the man. Stitch glanced at him, brown eyes the mirror of Kenzie's, minus any sign of softness.

"Carter," he said gruffly before turning back to the TV.

Carter fought back a sigh. "Uh . . . Noah said it's time to eat," he announced, trying to divert the attention away from himself. He was acutely aware of Kenzie watching from the other side of the room where she stood next to Violet and the tall, lanky form of Macon Bridges. Carter remembered him as a bit of a geek in high school—a quiet, non-intrusive guy into computers and video games— and thought he'd heard he got a scholarship to MIT or something equally impressive.

"Hey, Macon," he said, extending his hand. "Good to see you again."

Macon shook his hand with a bemused smile. "You say that like we don't see each other every day."

"Oh." Carter laughed nervously, trying to cover his blunder. "Well, it's still good to see you . . . as . . . you know . . . kind of a member of the family." He eyed Violet significantly and Macon flushed bright red. To Carter's surprise, Violet didn't glare at him. In fact, she didn't seem to notice him at all. Her rather dreamy gaze was focused only on Macon.

"Well, thanks," Macon replied with a nervous laugh. "Should we eat?" He took Violet's hand and pressed an absent kiss to the top of her head as the group moved into the dining room. Violet all but glowed under Macon's attentions, and Carter fought not to laugh out loud.

It appeared the tigress had been tamed.

Dinner was a loud affair. Carter, for the most part, was an observer. He listened closely, and learned a lot. Like Macon was a mechanic and owned his own garage only about a block from where Carter worked.

"What happened to MIT?" he asked before he could think better of it.

Macon shot him an odd look. "What do you mean?"

Carter cleared his throat, his cheeks heating as attention focused on him. How would he get himself out of this one?

"I mean, owning a garage is awesome," he said, fingers drumming on his thigh under the table. "I just thought you'd be an engineer or computer analyst or something, you know?" His voice drifted off at the general looks of confusion heading his way. "Because you're so smart, and uh..."

Macon's brow furrowed and he lifted his napkin to wipe his mouth. "Well, after MIT—"

So he did go.

"—I just decided that I'd rather work for myself than a big tech company. The garage gives me a decent living and time to develop my own projects."

"You should see the things Macon's working on," Violet gushed. "He's going to invent something amazing and change the world, I swear."

Macon blushed, but smiled at her shyly before turning back to Carter. "But we've talked about all of this before."

Crap. "Yeah, I know. Sorry . . . I just . . . forgot? For a minute?"

It was the worst excuse in the history of time, but Macon, nice guy that he was, let it go with a curious tip of his head and a nod.

Carter kept his mouth shut after that, and found out his father, David, was still at the hospital—chief of staff—and doing a little teaching as well. His mother did volunteer work with the senior center, as well as working with local foster families. Stitch Monroe was stoic as ever, speaking only occasionally to ask someone to pass the potatoes. His eyes softened when they lit on his grandchildren, however, and Carter could tell they were equally as crazy about him. Carter still wasn't completely certain what Noah and Lydia did—some kind of online business having to do with art—but they seemed to be doing well.

Carter absorbed the energy at the table, eating quietly and only interjecting when a question was addressed to him directly. He found himself laughing along with the others, however, enjoying the interactions between what was now his family.

It was almost perfect.

Except for the fact that he could feel the tension emanating from Kenzie where she sat next to him . . . the slight jerk every time her arm accidentally brushed his. The hurt and pain from her was almost palpable, and he wondered how no one else in the room noticed it.

Or maybe they could. Maybe they, like him, were glossing over it, trying to make the best of an uncomfortable situation . . . trying to ensure a happy holiday for his children.

As Lydia sliced the pumpkin pie, Carter let his eyes drift around the table. He smiled at Lydia and Noah, playfully arguing over how much whipped cream to put on each piece . . . to Violet and Macon, their heads together, talking in hushed tones as she squeezed his arm . . . to Stitch, who was having a heated discussion with Brady about whether Batman or Superman was the best superhero. On the other end of the table, his parents were smiling at Peyton as Claire wiped a smear of mashed potatoes off his daughter's chin. Then, of course, there was Kenzie.

Always Kenzie.

As his thoughts returned to the strained relationship with the woman who was now his wife, his smile fell.

What was he going to do?

He looked up as Lydia offered him a piece of pie, his hand trembling slightly when he passed it to Kenzie. She took it from him, but didn't take a bite.

How could he fix this?

Noah had told him he'd put other things— *everything* from what he could tell—before Kenzie. He supposed that he'd have to dig his way out of this mess the same way he got into it, bit by bit. He glanced at her out of the corner of his eye as she poked at her pie.

He'd have to show her that she was important to him . . . the *most* important thing to him.

He'd have to win her heart, romance her . . . *seduce* her. At that thought, he felt a telltale stirring under the table and grimaced at his inappropriate reaction.

Obviously, *that* would have to wait. He couldn't deny the fact that he wanted Kenzie. He wanted her badly. Even being this close to her was absolute torture . . . the smell of her hair . . . the warmth of her body.

But he couldn't screw this up, pardon the pun.

He'd all but lost her, and he'd have to heal the pain in her heart before he could even think about gaining access to her body.

He just prayed it wasn't too late.

Chapter
SEVEN
put one foot in front of the other

He slept on the couch.

When they'd arrived home after dinner, he'd helped Kenzie bathe the kids and put them to bed, enjoying the task more than he thought he would. When little Peyton wrapped her arms around his neck and rubbed her nose against his, his heart melted.

"'Night, Daddy," she said.

"'Night, Peyton."

"You've got to say it, Daddy," she said sleepily.

"Say what?"

"Good night, sweet dreams . . ." she began.

". . . my love is in the moonbeams," Carter concluded, remembering the rhyme his mother always recited at bedtime.

"That's right," she said on a yawn. "'Night, Daddy."

He leaned over and kissed her on the forehead. "'Night," he whispered.

He turned off the light as he left the room and made his way to Brady's bedside. Kenzie was sitting next to him, running her fingers through his hair.

"Can I ride my bike tomorrow?" he asked.

"If it isn't raining."

"I can ride in the rain."

"We'll see."

Brady frowned. "That means 'No.'"

Kenzie laughed and kissed his forehead. "That means *we'll see*. Now go to sleep."

"Okay."

Carter passed her as she left the room and leaned over the little boy. "I'll see you in the morning, buddy."

"Okay."

"Good night, sweet dreams . . ."

". . . my love is in the moonbeams," Brady finished, his eyes already drifting closed as Carter pulled the sheets to his chin and kissed the little boy's head.

He walked out into the hallway, only to see Kenzie standing in front of their room, her arms crossed over her chest. Carter stopped, his gaze dropping to the floor.

"I'll, uh, I'll just sleep downstairs."

Kenzie replied quietly. "I think that would be best."

"Can we talk tomorrow?"

"Don't you have to work?"

Did he? Carter had absolutely no idea.

"I'll be home by five," he said, a plan forming in his mind. "I want to take you out to a special dinner. I'll ask Lydia or my parents to watch the kids." He lifted hopeful eyes to Kenzie. She stared at him for a moment.

"Are you sure?" she asked tentatively. "You always say going out is a waste of money."

He did? What kind of idiot was he?

"It's a special occasion," he replied. "We need to talk, Kenzie. I . . . I don't want to lose you, and I'm willing to do whatever it takes for us to make things work." She began to speak, but he held up a hand to stop her.

"I know I've said this before, and I know actions speak louder than words," he continued. "So let me do this. Let me *show* you. Please?"

Kenzie took a deep breath, and for a moment, he thought she might deny him. Instead, she said one word in a small voice. One word that made hope swell inside him and a wave of relief rush through his body.

"Okay."

He smiled and turned to hop down the stairs, confidence beginning to blossom. He would show Kenzie the time of her life. It had been a while, but he still remembered how to win a woman over.

She wouldn't know what hit her.

He woke with a grunt to the feeling of Brady plopping down onto his stomach.

"Morning, Daddy," he said, bouncing slightly. "Did you fall asleep watching TV again?"

Carter winced at the reminder that he'd probably spent more than a few nights on the couch. "Uh, yeah. I guess I did."

"Mommy said it's time to get up!" Brady shouted, sliding back to the floor. "She's making pancakes!"

Carter's stomach growled as the scent of bacon reached his nostrils. "Sounds good," he rasped, sitting up and running his hands through his hair. "Tell her I'll be there in a minute, okay? I need to go get a shower."

"Okay!" Brady said gleefully, running into the kitchen.

Carter got up, stretching his aching muscles while yawning hugely. The night before, his mind had raced as he'd planned the big date, and he hadn't managed to fall asleep until long after midnight. He'd tossed and turned after that, partly due to the discomfort of sleeping on the couch . . . partly, he was sure, due to nerves over whether his plan would work.

He showered and dressed quickly, not wanting Kenzie to think he didn't appreciate her making breakfast. He did take the time to shave, however, tired of the beast growing on his chin. He scowled at his closet full of denim and flannel, wondering slightly at the absence of suits and ties. There was one dark gray suit, the elbows and knees shiny with age, and Carter decided he'd have to find time during the day to find something to wear for his date. He couldn't take Kenzie to dinner at *Aurora* dressed in plaid.

68

As for how to get a reservation at *Aurora* on such short notice . . . well, that was something he was going to have to address once he got to work. There were certain perks that came with working in the media. He hoped they also applied to small weekly newspapers on the Olympic Peninsula.

He slipped on a pair of worn boots and made his way downstairs and into the kitchen. He couldn't hold back a smile at the sight of the two children sitting at the breakfast bar. Brady was rolling his bacon up in his pancakes and dipping the roll into syrup before taking a bite. Peyton, apparently, didn't like syrup, opting to eat her pancakes dry. Kenzie looked up, handing him a cup of coffee, and her mouth dropped open.

"You shaved," she said.

"Um, yeah." He rubbed a hand over his now-smooth cheeks. His stomach sank at her stunned expression. "You don't like it?" Maybe she preferred the beard. Had he screwed up already?

"I don't know," she said finally. "You've had the beard for so long, I . . ." She blinked and shook her head. "It's fine." She looked away and wiped her hands on a towel. "Hungry?" she asked quietly.

"Starving."

"Have a seat."

Carter sat down next to Peyton, a little of the hesitancy from the day before reappearing. "Morning," he said quietly.

Peyton turned her hazel gaze on him briefly. "Morning, Daddy," she said, taking another bite of her pancake. "You look weird."

"I know." He cleared his throat. "Sorry."

She shrugged, chewing.

"Uh . . . how did you sleep?" he asked.

Peyton's brow creased in confusion. "In my bed."

Carter chuckled. "I meant, did you have good dreams?"

"Oh." Peyton shrugged, talking through another bite of pancake. "I don't 'member."

"I dreamed I was Superman!" Brady shouted, dipping his pancake roll in more syrup. "I was flying and I fought the bad guys!" He swung his fist to emphasize his story and inadvertently knocked over his milk.

"Brady," Kenzie chided, yanking a towel from the oven handle and blotting up the spill. "You need to be more careful."

"Sorry, Mommy," Brady replied. "You're not gonna cry, are you?"

Kenzie finished wiping up the milk and tossed the towel in the sink. "Why would I cry?"

"I don't know," Brady answered with a shrug. "But Grandma Claire says you shouldn't cry over spilled milk."

Kenzie laughed, and Carter felt his heart warm at the sound as he joined in. Kenzie caught his eye, and for the first time since he'd arrived the day before, a genuine smile lit her eyes before she turned back to Brady.

She tapped him on the nose. "I'm not going to cry," she assured him, pouring him some more milk. "Just try not to knock over your glass again, okay?"

Brady agreed, carefully picking it up to take a long swallow as Kenzie set a plate of pancakes and bacon in front of Carter.

"Thank you," he said quietly. Kenzie nodded in acknowledgement and moved to the sink to wash some dishes.

Carter finished his breakfast, and after a rather involved goodbye ritual with the kids, stood awkwardly in front of his wife.

"So, I'll be back at five," he promised.

"I'll be ready," she said. "Where are we going?"

"It's a surprise," he told her, seizing a moment of courage to lean in and kiss her cheek. He was grateful she didn't pull away.

"Just dress nice," he said. "I'll take care of everything."

Carter got into his car, clutching his business card in his hand as he started the little sedan. He made his way to the address of the *Woodlawn Weekly*, frowning slightly when he saw the small sign on a strip mall storefront.

"Well, it's no network news spot, but it's all mine," he said under his breath as he parked and made his way to the front door. A bell rang as he walked in, and an older woman sitting at a messy desk looked up, her eyes widening in surprise.

"What happened to you?"

"What?" Carter froze in front of the open door.

"Your face. It's bald."

"Oh, uh." He was ready to kick himself for shaving. "Just trying something new?"

"Well, you look real nice," the woman said after perusing him for a long moment. "Different, but nice."

She seemed familiar, and after a moment, Carter recognized her as the former secretary at Woodlawn High.

"Mrs. Evans?"

The woman laughed boisterously. "Mrs. Evans?" she repeated. "Since when have we gone back to that? I haven't been Mrs. Evans to you for years, Carter. Especially since you became my boss."

Carter forced a laugh. "Oh, just had a flashback, I guess . . ." He surreptitiously glanced at the nameplate on her desk. ". . . Sandi."

She giggled. "Oh, before I forget, Maddie wanted me to tell you she's up at the Rez covering the school board meeting. She said she'd drop by and get some pictures and quotes for the story on the new community center while she's there."

Carter nodded, his eyes drawn to a huge whiteboard on the wall behind Mrs. Evans'— *Sandi's*, he corrected—desk. Scrawled in dry erase marker was a list of the stories for the next issue, along with the reporters assigned to each story. From what he could tell, they were operating on a skeleton crew. No wonder he worked so much.

"Are you still heading up to Manaskat for the firefighter story?" she asked.

"Firefighter story?" he repeated.

Sandi rolled her eyes good naturedly. Apparently, absent-mindedness was not unusual for Carter. "The file's on your desk," she reminded him, "as well as the one for the food bank feature. You're set up for that one at one o'clock."

Carter started to panic. He had to drive to Manaskat, do the interviews for this firefighter story—whatever it was—as well as a food bank feature, find a suit, make reservations at the restaurant and the hotel, order flowers and a limo, as well as find some decent champagne in a town well known for its affinity for beer and peanuts. The list was growing by the minute.

He started to feel dizzy, wondering if he could pull it off.

"Carter, is everything all right?" Sandi asked, a concerned look wiping the pleasant smile from her face.

Carter rubbed his temple, feeling the beginnings of a headache. "It's just that . . . I hoped to plan a special night for Kenzie . . ."

Sandi's eyes softened. "That explains the new look. Is there anything I can do to help?"

Carter's eyes widened at the offer. "Could you? It would mean a lot to me."

She waved a hand. "It's no problem. So, you want a special table at The Mill?" She picked up the phone.

Carter frowned at the mention of Woodlawn's only nice restaurant. It was nowhere near nice enough for Kenzie. "No, I had something a little more special in mind." With that, he outlined his plan for Sandi Evans.

Sandi stared at him for a moment when he finally finished. "You want to do all of this *tonight?*" she asked.

"Yes. Can you do it?"

Sandi sighed heavily. "It'll take some doing, but yes, I think I can. You know this is going to cost a fortune, right?"

Carter smiled. "It's a special occasion." He reached into his pocket for his wallet, pulling out a credit card, then thinking the better of it and handing her three of them. "Just put it all on those," he said.

Feeling a weight lift off his shoulders, Carter made his way toward an office in the back of the room with a glass door boasting a brass placard declaring him Editor-in-Chief. He found the files Sandi had mentioned on top of a mountain of paperwork on his desk and flipped through them quickly. Evidently, the firefighter story was a look at the impact of budget cuts on the Wishkah County Fire District. The food bank feature was a typical story about the need for donations with the shelves pretty bare after the holiday rush. It all looked relatively cut and dried, and he felt he could easily get both stories done in the time allotted.

Until he actually got to Manaskat.

His phone rang non-stop on the drive and he spent most of the time on his headset, putting out fires at the printer and with other reporters in the field. He was exhausted by the time he pulled into the parking lot adjacent to the fire station, and finally had to shut his phone off when he sat down to do the interview with the fire chief and a few of the firefighters who'd had their hours cut back because of the budget cuts. He snapped a few pictures with his digital camera and headed for the only department store in town, turning on his phone to find he had seven voicemails.

He listened to them briefly, relieved when he found there was nothing pressing that couldn't wait until after he'd found a decent suit, which proved to be a little easier said than done. He scanned the racks, finally deciding on a dark gray one that fit him relatively well—no time for alterations—and a pair of black shoes that squeaked slightly, but looked pretty good. He opted for a white shirt and dark blue tie, since the selections were limited, and put the whole thing on the one credit card he'd held back from Mrs. Evans.

Carter had a moment of panic as he handed the card to the cashier, wondering if he had enough available on the card to cover the near-thousand dollar total. He breathed a sigh of relief when the young woman handed him the slip to sign and thanked him for his business. He put in a call to Sandi as he walked back to his car.

"How's it going?" he asked when she answered the phone.

"So far, so good," she said. "I got ahold of Lester Reynolds, and he'll meet you at the airport at five-thirty. I called in some favors and got you the okay to land on the ABC affiliate's helipad in Seattle. The limo will meet you there to take you to *Aurora.* The suite at the *Four Seasons* is reserved in your name, and Lester will be back to pick you up at nine in the morning."

"Thanks, Sandi. You're a miracle worker."

"I know," she said smugly. "Oh, and one thing?"

"Yes?"

"At *Aurora*," she said hesitantly. "They may be under the impression that you're a food critic from the *New York Times*."

"What?"

"Hey," Sandi replied, her voice taking on a defensive tone. "It was the only way I could get you a reservation so quickly. Plus, you'll probably get a few extras," she pointed out.

"Okay," Carter rubbed the bridge of his nose, wondering how he could pull off posing as a food critic.

"And the *Four Seasons* might be under the impression you're writing an article for *Conde Nast*," she added.

"Good Lord," Carter muttered.

"You ask for miracles, you've got to be willing to pay the price," she pointed out.

"It's . . . fine, Sandi. It's great. I really appreciate all your help."

"No problem," she said. "Just have a great time."

Carter hung up and checked his watch. With a low curse, he realized that he was already fifteen minutes late for his appointment at the food bank. He got into the car and turned the key.

And nothing happened.

"Come on," he encouraged the little car, as he turned the key again.

Nothing.

"No, no, no," he muttered, popping the hood and getting out of the car to stare at the engine.

Which was pretty much useless, since he knew virtually nothing about engines.

"Car trouble?" An older man paused on the sidewalk, peering in at the motor.

Carter fought back a sarcastic retort. "Yeah. It won't start. And I'm already late for an appointment."

The man leaned in, examining the engine closely and wiggling a few wires. "Try it now," he suggested.

Carter got back in the car and turned the key, hoping the wire-wiggling had fixed the problem.

It hadn't.

"Looks like a dead battery," the man said, pulling a handkerchief out of his pocket to wipe his hands. "I've got some cables in my truck. I'd be happy to give you a jump."

"Really?" Carter was shocked at the stranger's willingness to help him. It wasn't something that happened often in New York. "I'd really appreciate it."

"Sure, no problem," the man said, waving a hand in dismissal. "I'll go get my truck."

While Carter waited, he called the food bank to let them know what was happening, then scrolled through his phone numbers, breathing a relieved sigh when he found an entry for *Mom*. He placed a quick call to his mother, who was more than happy to take the children for the night, and Carter was thankful at least that hurdle had been cleared.

He waited for the man to return, checking his watch every few minutes. Finally, forty-five minutes later, a rickety old Ford pickup pulled up in front of him, the engine rattling loudly. Carter suppressed his irritation and pasted a smile on his face.

"Did you get lost?" he asked jokingly.

The man just blinked at him. "No," he said, before pulling a set of jumper cables out of the bed of his truck. He quickly hooked up to Carter's battery, and when the car started, Carter thanked him profusely before finally setting off toward the food bank. His foot anxiously pressed the gas pedal while his eyes scanned side streets and the rearview mirror, hoping to avoid getting a speeding ticket.

He pulled up in front of the food bank more than an hour late. He wasn't so much worried about the interview—the director was happy the paper was doing the story at all and bent over backward to accommodate Carter. But with the car trouble, Carter was on a tight schedule to get home in time to pick up Kenzie. He'd have to speed through the interviews, snap a few pictures, and get out of town as soon as possible.

Unfortunately, the schedule at the food bank was not quite as tight. He found the director, Jason Matthews, helping to unload a truckload of produce at the back door, and waited rather impatiently for him to finish.

"I can interview you right here," Carter offered, glancing at his watch again and wincing at the passing time.

"No, we'll be more comfortable in my office," Jason said. "This will only take a minute."

When Jason finally finished with the truck and led Carter to his office, it was almost three o'clock and Carter's teeth were on edge. Jason was a tedious interview—slow speaking, and Carter felt like he had to drag every quote from his lips. When he finally finished with him and the two food bank customers that Jason had recommended he interview as well, Carter was nearly frantic. He took a few pictures of the empty shelves as well as the outside of the facility before practically running to his car. It was after four o'clock. He barely had time to get home and change before they needed to meet Lester at the airport.

Of course, the car wouldn't start.

"Damn it!" Carter exclaimed, pounding on the steering wheel in frustration. He still needed to get flowers on the way home, and his battery was dead again. "You stupid! Stupid! Car!"

"Having trouble, Carter?" Jason's face appeared at his passenger side window, his voice muffled by the glass.

Carter rolled down the window, fighting to control his frustration and smile hopefully at the man.

"Got any jumper cables?" he asked.

CHAPTER
EIGHT

all i want for christmas is you

B y the time Jason and Carter managed to get his car started, Carter was in a near panic. He called Kenzie, getting her voicemail, and assured her he was on his way, and would be there as soon as possible. He left the car running when he dashed into a small florist shop to pick up a bouquet of red roses. He knew they were cliché, but didn't have any other options.

Finally . . . *finally*, he sped down Highway 160, his eyes compulsively drifting to the dashboard clock. No matter how many times he looked at it, it still told him the same thing.

He was late.

He'd called Sandi and asked her to contact Lester and let him know what was happening. Things weren't going quite as planned, but Carter was determined not to let the day's events ruin everything.

Carter's new suit slid off the back of the passenger seat and he reached over to straighten it quickly. He had no time for a shower, that was for sure. He sniffed at himself. Not too bad. A quick spritz of cologne ought to do the job.

His gaze flicked back to the suit. He had wanted to be wearing it when he picked up Kenzie—not running through the front door in a crazed hurry to change.

Kind of ruined the romance.

He eyed the suit speculatively, then examined the empty road ahead of him.

He could pull over and change, but it would be much quicker to just do it while he was driving. His eyes narrowed at the plastic-wrapped garment next to him. The shirt and tie would be no problem. He was already wearing dark socks, and changing shoes would be easy.

The pants, though. The pants could prove challenging.

"Heck with it," he muttered, reaching over with one hand to unbutton the shirt and pull it off the hanger. Of course, the jacket came with it and Carter cursed lightly as he shook the shirt free, then draped the jacket over the seat back. He only bothered to release the top two buttons on the shirt he was wearing before quickly tugging it over his head, the car swerving slightly. Gritting his teeth, he threw the flannel over his shoulder before slipping an arm into the crisp, white shirt. He leaned forward, his left arm flailing behind him as he tried to find the sleeve opening, the seatbelt cutting across his neck. By the time he managed to get his arm in the sleeve he was damp with sweat. He tried to pull the shirt up onto his shoulders.

It just . . . wouldn't . . . *move*.

"Come on!" he exclaimed in frustration. After a few more wiggles and a desperate yank he feared would tear the seams, he realized he'd managed to twist the shirt behind him. He was now trapped in some kind of white cotton straightjacket of doom.

Carter realized he was quickly closing in on the Woodlawn city limits and decided to quit while he was behind and pull over at the next opportunity. He spotted a wide spot on the shoulder and stopped there in relief. He would have preferred something a little more hidden from the road, but traffic was light, and he didn't really see any better options.

Carter quickly released his seatbelt and managed to break free of his shirt prison with a victorious grunt. He pulled the shirt on and shimmied out of his jeans, reaching for the new pants and glancing at his watch simultaneously. If he hurried, they'd still make their reservation at *Aurora*.

Carter tossed the jeans into the back seat and glanced into the rearview mirror just in time to see a flash of red and blue.

Red and blue lights.

As in . . . lights on a police car.

With a groan, Carter scrambled to jam his legs into the suit pants, yanking them up over his thighs just as an officer tapped on the window with the end of his flashlight.

Carter readied a sheepish smile and looked up . . . only to come face to face with the one person he pretty much never wanted to meet with his pants down.

That's right. Sheriff Jeremiah "Stitch" Monroe.

A phrase involving *deer, headlights*, and rather colorful profanity ran through Carter's mind.

He rolled down the window. "Hi, Sheriff," he said, deciding to play it off as a joke. It was his father-in-law, after all.

"Carter," Stitch replied, his pointed gaze taking in Carter's disheveled appearance. "License and registration."

Kenzie's father never did like him much. Figured that wouldn't change, even in an alternate reality. Of course, he *was* half-naked on the side of the road.

Carter fumbled in his pants pockets, realizing his wallet was in the jeans he'd thrown into the back of the car. He swallowed thickly, then turned and bent over the seat, pulling his pants up over his butt as he moved. He retrieved the wallet and handed his license and registration to the sheriff.

Stitch Monroe, face devoid of emotion, examined the documents, then eyed Carter suspiciously. "You want to tell me what you're doing, Carter?"

Carter forced a laugh. "Funny story," he began, but at the sheriff's deadpan expression, he decided on another tact.

"I was trying to surprise Kenzie," he said instead. "I'm taking her to a nice dinner tonight, and I'm running late. I thought it might be easier to change in the car."

Carter swore he saw the sheriff's lips quirk slightly. Of course he might have imagined that.

"How's that working for you?" he asked.

"Uh . . . not so good," Carter replied, buttoning up his shirt and tucking it into his pants quickly as he reached for his tie. "Do you think you could let me off with a warning? I really want to get to Kenzie."

Stitch's face took on a dark look. "She does deserve a night out. Especially after what happened Christmas Eve."

Carter's heart sank. Did everyone know about that? The ever-grinding gossip mill was one thing he didn't miss about small towns.

"Well, uh, I really want to try and make it up to her."

"You should."

The sheriff stood silently for a moment, and Carter wondered if he was going to let him go, or haul him in for questioning.

Or torture. It wasn't outside the realm of possibility.

The sheriff tapped the butt of his flashlight against his open palm, his eyes impassive, and Carter swallowed thickly.

Fortunately, Stitch had mercy on his son-in-law, and with a few gruff words and a warning not to change on the side of the road again, he handed the license and registration back to Carter and turned to head back to his cruiser.

Carter breathed a heavy sigh and adjusted his tie, examining it in the rearview mirror. He saw Stitch watching him, and quickly reached for the key.

In a perfect world, the car would have started and Carter would have made it home in time to whisk Kenzie away to a beautiful dinner at a four-star restaurant.

In *Carter's* world, the car wouldn't start, he had to ask his father-in-law—who apparently hated his guts—to give him a jump, and when he finally got home he was in such a rush that he slammed the roses in the car door.

Kenzie, to her credit, smiled prettily when he offered the slightly crushed flowers to her. She wore a green silky dress that wrapped around her slender frame and swayed hypnotically when she moved. Carter hadn't been able to speak and thrust the roses toward her, like a teenager on his first date.

"I, uh, had some trouble with the flowers. And the car door," he explained lamely as several wilted petals drifted to the floor.

Kenzie laughed. "Well, they're beautiful. Thank you."

Carter followed her into the kitchen, trying not to be obvious when he glanced at his watch. Fortunately, his mother had already picked up the children, but Carter knew they needed to get going.

"Are you ready?" he asked Kenzie as she filled a vase and began arranging the less-damaged flowers.

"Hmm?"

Carter cleared his throat. "Are you ready to go? We have a reservation."

She hurriedly stuck the rest of the flowers into the vase, adjusting them as she frowned. "Okay," she said, drying her hands on a towel. "Let me get my coat."

They managed to get out of the house and into the minivan—Carter wasn't going to rely on his untrustworthy battery for such an important night—and headed out of town.

"Where are we going?" Kenzie asked. "I thought we were heading to *The Mill*."

Carter smiled enigmatically. "It's a surprise." He was pleased to see Kenzie flush a little in pleasure as he watched her out of the corner of his eye while they approached the airport.

"Carter?" She looked at him questioningly as he parked the van and jogged around to open the door and help her out.

"Just come on," he said quietly, taking her hand in his. The feel of her soft skin against his made him feel warm and slightly giddy. He led her across the tarmac to where Lester was completing a pre-flight check on his helicopter.

Kenzie came to an abrupt stop. "We're not going up in that," she stated, shaking her head slowly.

Carter tugged on her arm. "It'll be fun. Come on."

"Fun?" she repeated, turning panicked eyes to him. "Carter, those things are dangerous. And Lester Reynolds?" Her voice lowered to a whisper. "You know that guy's a nutjob!"

"Relax, Kenzie. I've flown in these a million times," he assured her.

"You have? When?" Kenzie asked, confused.

Carter faltered. *In another life. In another world.*

"Okay, you got me," he admitted after a moment. "Maybe not a million times, but believe me, it's perfectly safe."

"I don't know," she said hesitantly.

"Come on, Kenzie . . . please." He turned a pleading gaze on her, hoping she was still susceptible to it. "I have an amazing evening planned, but we need to get in that helicopter to make it happen."

Kenzie bit her lip, eyeing the chopper warily. When she released her lip, Carter knew he'd won.

"Okay. Let's go."

They ran toward the helicopter and Lester helped them both in, handing them headsets before starting the rotor.

"Just relax," Lester said with a grin, his voice tinny over the headset. "You'll be in Seattle in no time."

"How long have you been flying, Lester?" Kenzie asked, her voice cracking nervously.

Lester laughed, exchanging a few words with the tower before pulling the stick and launching them off the ground. "Longer than you've been alive, sweetie," he said. "Used to make supply runs in 'Nam before I took some shrapnel to my knee." He rubbed his leg for a moment. "Ferrying tourists around the Peninsula isn't the same as dodging mortar fire, but . . ." His voice trailed off almost longingly at the thought of his war years and Kenzie exchanged a significant look with Carter.

See? she seemed to say with her eyes. *Nutjob!*

Carter stifled a chuckle.

They landed in Seattle and Kenzie was sufficiently awed at the sleek black limousine waiting for them. Carter found a bottle of champagne chilling inside the vehicle and mentally thanked Sandi for her foresight as he poured them both a glass.

Kenzie sipped at the bubbly liquid. "I haven't had champagne since Lydia and Noah's wedding," she said. "That didn't go so well."

Carter just laughed as if he knew what she was talking about.

"Hopefully, you won't have to hold my hair this time," she continued, shedding some light on what must have happened at his sister's wedding.

Carter smiled warmly. "I would, you know," he replied earnestly. "I'd do anything for you, Kenzie."

He worried Kenzie might find the sentiment corny, but she smiled—a real smile—and Carter's heart soared. It was working. She would forgive him and they would be happy.

Finally.

CHAPTER NINE

silent night

They pulled up to the front of the restaurant and the driver quickly rounded the limo to open the car door with a flourish. This time it was Kenzie who slipped her hand into Carter's as they approached the glass entrance of the angular wood and stone structure. Carter held the door for Kenzie to enter, pressing his hand lightly to her lower back as they took in the flickering firelight coming from the stone fireplace, and the incredible views in the dining room beyond.

"This is amazing, Carter," Kenzie whispered, once the waitress had left them with ice water and a bread basket. She turned to look out the floor-to-ceiling windows at the sparkling lights of Seattle reflecting off the surface of Lake Union below them.

"Don't get me wrong," she continued, "I appreciate it—really—but how can we afford all this?"

"Don't worry about it," Carter replied dismissively, buttering a piece of bread. He didn't notice Kenzie's frown at his response, and the arrival of the waitress ended the conversation for the moment.

The meal was exquisite, and enormous. Carter had only ordered a prawn appetizer for the two of them to share and Colorado lamb chops with couscous, while Kenzie opted for the sablefish with matsutake mushrooms and bok choy. However, the waitress kept bringing them other dishes to sample. When Carter protested that he hadn't ordered them, the waitress simply smiled and said they were on the house. Foie gras, yellow fin tuna, steak tartare, gnocchi with black truffles . . . the list went on and on, and Carter soon lost track of what they'd eaten. Although he understood that this was because of the cover story Sandi had concocted about him being a food critic, Kenzie just laughed and marveled at their amazing luck. The owner of the restaurant even stopped by to make sure they were happy with their meal. He also presented them with a complimentary bottle of champagne as they enjoyed their dessert samplers of crème brulee, Grand Marnier soufflé, and some kind of doughnuts with passion fruit-vanilla cream, coconut, and macadamia nuts.

Carter briefly contemplated a change in career. How hard could it be to be a food critic, anyway?

They left the restaurant with their stomachs full, a little tipsy, and laughing at the most ridiculous things. The limo was waiting for them, and as they tumbled into the seat, Carter lost his balance, falling onto Kenzie. He found himself sprawled over her, his left knee pressed between hers and their faces so close he could feel her warm breath on his lips.

He froze, wondering if she would protest, and unable to move until he found out. She said nothing, her eyes dipping to his lips before she licked her own slowly and brought her gaze back to meet his. He leaned closer, almost near enough to taste her mouth . . . waiting to see if she would stop him.

She didn't.

Carter cheered inwardly, the man who'd longed for Kenzie Monroe for ten long years finally breathed a sigh of relief as their lips brushed gently.

"Kenzie," he murmured into her mouth, as she opened it on a sigh. He took it as an invitation and swept his tongue inside, shivering at the sensation as it slid sinuously along hers. She tasted of coconut and vanilla and champagne. Carter fought to not consume her, afraid he'd scare her and he'd have to stop kissing her.

He never wanted to stop.

Kenzie seemed to feel the same way. She tilted her head to deepen the kiss, her hands sweeping up his arms to settle on the back of his neck, massaging him gently. He moaned at the sensation, sliding his arms underneath her to pull her more firmly against him. He was rewarded by Kenzie's gentle whimper and the tightening of her fingers in his hair. Carter caressed her soft skin and mouthed

at the tender spot beneath her ear that always used
to drive her crazy.

It still did.

They made out like teenagers, all teeth and
tongue and moaning and groping . . . grinding
against each other in a frenzy of lust and
champagne-fueled loss of inhibition.

"God, Carter . . ." Kenzie ripped the tails of his
shirt from his pants and thrust her hands
underneath, raking her nails up and down his back.
Carter threw his head back, reveling in the
sensation as he pulled Kenzie's hips even tighter
against his own. He lowered his head to her neck,
nuzzling and kissing a trail along her shoulder as
she trembled beneath him.

As the limo came to a stop, their passion
slowed, and he held her close, a heated gentleness
passing through him that had less to do with lust,
and everything to do with love.

God, he loved her.

The door slammed and Carter realized they'd
arrived at the hotel. He quickly got up, shielding
Kenzie from the door as he straightened her dress,
ignoring his own disheveled appearance. Her eyes
drifted halfway open as a sleepy smile lit her face.

"We're here," he said quietly.

Kenzie blinked, then sat up just as the driver
opened the passenger door. Carter took her hand
with a wide smile and led her through the huge iron
gates and front gardens of the Four Seasons Hotel,
then under the awning and into the spacious
interior.

"What are we doing here?" Kenzie asked, her face still slightly dazed, as if she'd just realized where they were. The champagne and the make-out session had evidently done a number on her.

Carter leaned in to kiss her cheek. "Wait here just a minute," he said, before approaching the check-in desk. He glanced back at Kenzie to find her biting her lip nervously as she surveyed the paneled walls, rich carpeting, and leather furniture mixed with luscious, dark fabrics. She caught his eye, smiling weakly, and Carter wondered if she was nervous . . . if he was assuming too much by taking her to a hotel.

Of course, he realized they were married and had slept together many times. But since he'd arrived, the tension between them made it apparent that those times had been fewer and farther between lately. And the encounter in the limo was the first time he'd really had a taste of Kenzie in that way.

He wanted more than a taste. He wanted the entire banquet.

He swallowed thickly and turned back to the desk clerk, fighting down the animalistic urges that pushed at his control. Tonight was about winning Kenzie back. Not just getting her into bed.

Still, he would have been lying to say he didn't have high hopes that would be part of the package.

Palming the room key, Carter crossed to Kenzie and wrapped an arm around her waist as they turned toward the elevators.

"Carter, this really isn't necessary," she whispered. "We have a perfectly good bed at home."

Carter laughed as they entered the elevator and ascended to their floor. Kenzie shifted nervously on her feet, her face flushing.

"Are you okay?" he asked.

"Carter . . ." she began, but the opening of the elevator doors interrupted whatever she was going to say. He took her hand, pulling her down the hallway toward their corner suite. Opening the door with a flourish, he watched Kenzie's face as she took in the room and her breath caught in her throat.

A sitting area was set up in front of a massive bay window looking out over the city lights. Palm fronds swayed in the slight breeze from the heater vents, giving the room a glamorous, old-Hollywood feel. A fire burned in the fireplace off to the side, next to a gleaming wooden desk sporting yet another bottle of champagne on ice. Through a set of double doors to the left of the sitting area, a king-sized bed with white linens, piles of pillows, and a puffy cloud of a duvet beckoned.

Carter felt it calling to him personally.

Kenzie took a few steps into the room and spun in a slow circle, taking it all in.

"Carter. This is too much," she said, her voice awed.

"No," he replied, moving toward her and taking her in his arms. "Nothing's too much for you."

"That's sweet, really. But all of this . . . for just a few hours . . ."

Unable to resist, he leaned in to kiss her neck, nuzzling her hair to inhale her scent. "We have all night. There's no rush."

"What?"

His lips trailed along the neckline of her dress. "We have all night. Then room service in the morning. And I thought we'd spend the day exploring the city." He nibbled at her collarbone. "Or we could stay here, if you want. We don't have to leave the room."

Suddenly she pushed him away. "We can't stay here all night."

"Why not?" he asked, reaching for her. "My mom's happy to keep the kids. You know that."

"You really don't remember, do you?" Kenzie's face was flushed, her eyes flashing. Carter suddenly realized that what he'd identified as nerves, was in fact, anger.

She was *furious.*

And he had absolutely no idea why.

"What's wrong?" he asked, his stomach sinking. "Remember what?"

Kenzie pushed her hair back from her face before letting her arms fall to her sides in defeat. "The writing seminar, Carter? I've only been talking about it for months."

Carter opened his mouth, but no words came out. He didn't know what to say.

"God, Carter," she said with something close to disgust. "It was one day—*one day.* All I asked was for you to watch the kids so I could go to this seminar. You know how important this is to me!"

"Well," Carter floundered. "You can still go. We'll head home first thing in the morning."

"It's in *Portland*, Carter!" she countered. "I was going to have to get up at five in the morning to drive down. I could have left from here if we'd brought the car, but that's not even the point."

"Well, what *is* the point?" he replied, feeling a surge of his own anger. He was only trying to create a romantic evening, and all she could give him was a load of grief.

"The point, Carter," she said through gritted teeth, "is that you didn't even *remember*. You made all of these plans and now I'm a horrible person for ruining them."

"You're not a horrible person."

"Well, I *feel* like one," she said angrily. "I *feel* like I'm supposed to forget about the seminar and tell you it's not a big deal. Yet again, what I want . . . what I *need* is disregarded. What's important to me doesn't even matter to you!"

"That's not true." Carter stuck his chin out stubbornly.

"No?" Kenzie retorted. "What about U-Dub?"

"What?"

Kenzie rolled her eyes. "I was ten credits and a thesis away from my Master's . . . *ten credits*, Carter."

"So? That's my fault?" he countered, getting frustrated at her attitude, despite the fact that he didn't even know what she was talking about.

"No, it's not your fault," she said sarcastically. "But you didn't exactly make it easy for me to go back and finish."

"You could have done it if you really wanted to." He crossed his arms over his chest, unsure if he was correct, but too swept up in the argument to care.

"How, Carter?" she replied, her eyes glassy with unshed tears. "With two kids? With a mortgage and a car payment? With you off chasing your dream of starting your own paper?"

"My dream?" Carter repeated with a choked laugh. "You think a weekly paper in Woodlawn is *my* dream? Yeah, right, Kenzie, because covering Walmart openings and the local elementary school Christmas pageant is the height of investigative journalism!"

"Oh, so it all comes back to this again."

"To what?"

"To what?" She threw her hands up, then scrubbed them over her face in frustration. "To New York, that's what. You've never forgiven me for missing that internship."

"I . . . I what?" Carter pinched the bridge of his nose, his eyes clenched tight. How was he supposed to argue that point when he had no idea if it was true? He couldn't imagine resenting Kenzie for not taking the internship. Of course, he really didn't understand why he didn't take it in the first place.

"I should have gone," he said quietly.

"I can't believe you said that."

"If I would have gone, I would have had a better job. I could have provided for you and the kids better. You would have been able to finish your Master's."

"Kids? There wouldn't have *been* any kids, Carter. You would have been in New York and I would have been here. We decided *together* that you'd stay here and take the job at the *Times*. You said you wanted to be with me."

"I do want to be with you," he said.

"Then why do you keep throwing that decision back in my face?"

"Why do you keep bringing up your Master's?"

Kenzie paused, breathing heavily for a moment before she collapsed on the lavish sofa, her face falling into her hands. "I can't keep doing this," she said in a near whisper.

Carter rubbed the back of his neck, trying to ease the tension there. He approached Kenzie, all anger gone, and fell to his knees in front of her.

"I'm sorry, Kenzie."

"You're always sorry, Carter. I'm sorry, too." She sat back eyeing him steadily. "How did we get here? Resenting each other . . . ignoring each other?"

Carter reached tentatively for her hand and stroked the back of it gently. "I don't know. We can get back, though, can't we? Can't we at least try?"

Kenzie smiled sadly at him, but said nothing.

They rented a car and drove home in silence, without even the radio to bridge the gap between them. Exhausted, Kenzie fell asleep curled up against the back of the seat, her soft breaths a counter-rhythm to the monotonous drone of tires on pavement. Carter glanced at her often as he maneuvered the nearly empty highway, wishing he could find some answers.

His romantic night had turned into a disaster, and he had no idea how to fix it. The ten years they'd been together—the ten years he'd *missed*—had somehow damaged what they'd once had.

Still . . . it wasn't dead.

Carter knew he was still in love with Kenzie. He had no doubt of it. And deep down, he knew that Kenzie still loved him, too.

She was hurt, angry, and frustrated, but she still loved him.

He would have to find a way to make it up to her. A way to show her they still had a chance. He just had no idea exactly how to do it.

chapter TEN

my true love gave to me

"I thought I knew what I was doing, but I had no clue," Carter told Noah once they'd dropped off the rental car in Manaskat. Kenzie had left early in the morning to head to Portland for her writing seminar, leaving Carter with the kids and a Volvo that had to be back at the car rental place by noon. Noah had agreed to drive Carter's car so he'd have a way home. They'd stopped by Macon's garage before they left Woodlawn, and he'd given Carter a good deal on a new battery, so he was hopeful he could avoid jumper cables for a while.

The kids had spotted the famous Golden Arches, prompting a stop at McDonald's to play in the tubes, slides, and ball pit in between bites of Chicken McNuggets and fries.

"It was going so well," Carter continued, eyeing Brady as he dipped a nugget in some ketchup. "Then I ended up on the couch. *Again.*"

"Ouch." Noah winced. "So, all that build up and you didn't even get to have . . ." He glanced at the kids. " . . . uh . . . *pillows*?" he said significantly, evidently trying to speak in code to avoid uncomfortable questions.

Carter laughed humorlessly, munching on a French fry. "Nope. No *pillows* for me. Not even a little one."

"How long has it been since you've had . . . a pillow?" Noah asked.

"I can't even remember," Carter said honestly.

Brady smiled brightly. "You can use my pillow, Daddy. I have two!"

Carter smiled, ruffling his son's hair. "Thanks, buddy."

"I'm done," Brady announced. "Can I go play some more?"

Carter nodded. "Watch out for Peyton, okay?"

"I will," he said, taking his little sister's hand and leading her to the ball pit. Carter's eyes never left them, a paternal protectiveness he never knew he possessed taking over. He spoke to Noah, but didn't look away from his children.

"I just don't know what she wants," he admitted to his brother-in-law. "I thought if I took her out for a night on the town . . . showed her how important she was to me, it would be enough, but . . ." He shrugged, draggin a fry listlessly through a blob of ketchup.

"That's rough, man," Noah said through a mouthful of burger. He swallowed and took a sip of his Coke. "What are you going to do now?"

101

"I'm not sure," Carter replied, picking at the bun on his own burger and half-smiling as Brady gently tossed a red ball to Peyton. "Maybe I should get her something pretty. Women like jewelry, right?"

Noah laughed. "If my wife is any indication, I'd say yes, women like jewelry." He sobered slightly. "But I don't know if that's what the situation calls for, Carter. Kenzie's not really one for fancy things."

"But she *should* be," Carter countered. "She should have every beautiful thing. And I should be the one to give them to her."

"Well, it's worth a try, I guess," Noah said doubtfully. "But I don't know that throwing money at the problem is really the solution."

"It's not about throwing money at it," Carter replied stubbornly. "It's about showing Kenzie how special she is."

Noah shrugged and wished his friend luck.

They dropped Noah off at his parents' house on the north side of town. He said Lydia would meet him there later, and he'd ride home with her. Carter and the kids set out to find a jewelry store that sold more than turquoise and friendship bracelets. They finally found a little shop squeezed between a bookstore and a specialty tea shop that looked promising.

With a firm admonishment not to touch anything, Carter walked into the store, holding his children's hands tightly in each of his own.

"Can I help you find something?" An older woman wearing a sequined snowman sweater popped up from behind the counter. She smiled down at Brady and Peyton. "Oh, what adorable children!" she exclaimed. "Would you two like a candy cane?"

The kids looked up at Carter for permission before nodding slowly. The woman bent down to hand them each a little candy cane and touched their cheeks gently. "So much like my own grandchildren," she mused. "Don't get to see them much since my son and his family moved to Phoenix." She sighed heavily, then shook her head.

"Enough about me," she said, standing up quickly. "What can I help you with today?"

Carter winced slightly. "I'm not exactly sure. I'd like to find something for my wife."

The woman chuckled. "In the doghouse, huh?"

"Something like that."

Brady tugged on his father's sleeve, pulling out his candy cane to whisper. "Daddy, we don't have a doghouse."

The saleslady burst out laughing. "Oh, he's a cute one!" she said, touching his cheek again. "Say, what's your name?"

"Brady."

"And your sister?"

"Peyton."

"Well, Brady, if it's okay with your daddy, I have a few toys back behind the counter over there." She pointed to where she'd been standing when they walked in. "You can take Peyton over there to play while I help your daddy find a present for your mom."

Once again, Brady looked up at Carter for permission. Carter didn't understand the warm swelling he felt in his heart at the boy's hopeful gaze.

"It's okay. Go ahead," Carter encouraged him. Brady took his sister's hand and led her behind the counter. He could see them pull a couple of little trucks from a basket of toys and begin running them along the floor.

"Thanks," Carter said, "Mrs. . . ."

The woman waved a hand. "Oh, just call me Gwen," she said.

"I'm Carter."

"Fine . . . fine, Carter," Gwen said cheerfully. "Now, you want something for your lovely wife. Maybe a necklace . . . or a nice bracelet?"

Carter's eyes ran over the glittering pieces nestled in black velvet under glass. "I think . . . something simple?" he said, more as a question than a statement.

Gwen nodded, tapping her fingers against her lips as she thought. She rounded the counter, unlocked a sliding panel, and pulled out one of the velvet trays. She picked up a silver bracelet made up of delicate links. A heart-shaped charm dangled from the chain, glinting in the dim light.

"We can engrave her name on the charm while you wait," Gwen told him. "We could even set the heart with the children's birthstones if you'd like . .

104

. make it a little more special. That would take a few hours, though."

"Really?" Carter asked, reaching out to touch the little silver charm. "How much?"

Gwen told him, and after only a brief hesitation, Carter nodded, reaching for his wallet and his now well-used credit card. He wondered what his limit was and once again held his breath while she ran it through, only releasing it when she handed the sales slip for him to sign.

"Now," she said, handing him a receipt. "Which birthstones do you need?"

Carter blanched. He had absolutely no idea. "I, uh, I don't know."

Gwen laughed. "Oh, most men don't," she said. "Just give me their birthdays and I can figure it out."

Crap. How could he explain to this woman that he didn't know his own children's birthdays? Yeah. That'd get him nominated for Father of the Year for sure.

Brady chose that moment to approach, reaching for his father's hand. Carter leaned down to pick him up, seeing an opportunity to redeem himself, or at least cover his ignorance.

"Brady," he said. "Can you tell the nice lady your birthday?"

Brady smiled. "I'm gonna be seven!"

"That's lovely," Gwen replied, reaching out to ruffle his hair. "When's your birthday?"

"February eighth," he said proudly, stumbling slightly over the pronunciation of "February."

"February," Gwen repeated. "That's amethyst. What about your sister?"

Brady frowned. "I don't know."

Carter's stomach fell. Quickly, he reached in his pocket. "My phone," he said apologetically, hoping the woman believed he had it on vibrate. "I'll just be a second."

Gwen nodded as Carter set Brady on the floor by his sister and the little boy went back to playing with trucks. Carter said *hello* like he was answering the phone, and when Gwen looked away, he quickly dialed Noah's number.

"Hello?"

"Noah," Carter whispered, walking to the far end of the store. "When's Peyton's birthday?"

"Carter?"

Carter rolled his eyes. "Yes . . . yes, it's Carter. I need your help."

"What's wrong?"

"I need to know Peyton's birthday."

"You don't remember her birthday?" Noah asked, his voice laced with confusion.

Carter sighed in frustration, pinching the bridge of his nose and fighting to speak quietly. "Please, Noah . . . just . . . humor me, okay?"

"Carter, what is *wrong* with you?"

"Noah!" Carter shouted into the phone, and catching Gwen's surprised expression, quickly forced a smile and lowered his voice. "Help me out here."

"Okay . . . okay," Noah replied. "It's April fourteenth. Carter, are you sure you're okay?"

106

Carter released a heavy breath. "I don't know, man."

"Can I help?"

"You just did," he said. "Seriously. I'll be fine. I'll talk to you later, okay?"

"Sure," Noah said, huffing slightly. "If you ever decide to tell me what's going on, I'll be around."

"I know, man," Carter replied quietly. "I'm just . . . dealing with some stuff. Really. I'll be fine."

"Okay," he said slowly, evidently not buying it.

"Bye, Noah . . . and thanks."

"No problem."

Carter hung up the phone and walked back over to add a little diamond to Kenzie's bracelet.

"I have something for you," Carter said enthusiastically when Kenzie walked in the door. It was late and the kids were in bed, but he was so excited about his gift he couldn't sleep. He waited in the living room, listening for the sound of the minivan pulling into the driveway. When he finally heard it, he was nearly vibrating with excitement. He felt confident that his thoughtful gift would get him back in Kenzie's good graces.

Kenzie yawned in the entryway, tugging her coat from her shoulders tiredly. "Something for me?"

Carter jumped up to help her with her coat. "You look exhausted," he said. "How was the seminar?"

Kenzie smiled, but it didn't reach her eyes. Apparently their argument from the night before hadn't been forgotten. "It was great," she said quietly. "Jackson McKay is an amazing writer, and I learned a lot from him. He's actually going to be teaching a writing class in Manaskat that starts in a couple of weeks. He suggested I take it." She watched Carter closely, gauging his reaction.

Carter smiled at her. "That's fantastic. I think you should do it."

"You do?"

Carter felt mystified and a little ashamed at the shock in her voice. Did she really think he'd fight her on this? Obviously, in the past he would have. He found himself growing increasingly irritated with his alter ego.

What a jerk.

"You didn't even ask how much it would cost," she said.

"We'll make it work." Carter shrugged.

"It'll be two nights a week for a month," she added. "I'd drive up right after work and you'd have to handle the kids . . . dinner . . . baths . . . bed . . . all of it."

"I can do that."

"Wow," Kenzie said, a smile lighting her face. "Who are you, and what have you done with Carter?"

Carter laughed, pulling her to the couch. "I just want you to know that I support you in whatever you do," he said earnestly. "I love you, Kenzie. I'm sorry about last night. About everything."

Kenzie felt tears prick her eyes. "I'm sorry, too."

Carter picked up the gift wrapped box from where it lay on the coffee table. "I got this for you today," he said. "I want you to know how important you are to me, Kenzie. I know I haven't shown it much lately, but things have really changed. *I've* changed. I want . . . I *need* for you to understand that things will be different from now on."

He handed her the little box, and she took it slowly, running her fingers over the gold ribbon. "It's so pretty," she said quietly.

"Open it."

Her eyes flashed to his briefly before returning to the box. She tugged on the bow, pulling it from the package, then slid her finger under the wrapping to remove it. She hesitated for a moment before lifting the lid.

"Oh, Carter," she breathed, lifting it from the box and studying the little heart-shaped charm that now said *Kenzie* in elegant script, accented by two little gemstones.

"They're the kids' birthstones," he pointed out.

Kenzie nodded. "I see that. It's . . . it's beautiful, Carter. But it's too much. How can we afford this?" She lifted her hesitant gaze to his.

Carter waved off her concerns. "Don't worry about it."

Kenzie's brow creased. "But, Carter, after last night—the helicopter ride and dinner . . . and that hotel suite, and now this. It had to cost a fortune."

He leaned in and kissed her forehead indulgently. "I said, don't worry about it," he repeated.

Kenzie's face tensed. "But where is the money coming from?"

Carter felt a twinge of irritation. "Kenzie, can't you just enjoy the gift? Why are you making such a big deal about this? I've got it covered. Can't you just trust me?"

Kenzie frowned for a moment, biting her lip. "Of course, I trust you," she said finally, worry still evident on her face. "It's a beautiful bracelet, Carter. Thank you."

"You're welcome."

She put the lid back on the box. She didn't say anything more about the money, but Carter could sense the issue wasn't settled.

"I'm really tired," she said, standing up slowly and not meeting his eyes. "The kids will be up early tomorrow. I'm going to go to bed."

Carter waited for her to invite him to go with her, but she didn't. Instead, she leaned over to kiss him softly on the cheek.

"Thank you again," she said politely. "Good night."

"Good night," Carter replied, trying to hide his disappointment. He'd been so hopeful that the bracelet would help him turn a corner with Kenzie, but he had the strangest feeling that it might have actually made things worse. He slipped off his shoes, and stretched out on the sofa, then sat up again to pull his wallet and keys from his pocket.

When he saw the little silver bell resting in his palm, he considered it carefully.

Henry had told him only to use it for emergencies. He wondered if not knowing what was going through his wife's mind would qualify.

Or an epic case of sexual frustration.

Or a desire to sleep on a real bed instead of a lumpy sofa.

He looked at the bell for a long time, weighing the pros and cons of ringing it and maybe getting a few answers to help him along the way. But, he couldn't fight the feeling that maybe he needed to hold off . . . that he might need Henry more at another time and he needed to save his last two bell rings for even more desperate times.

His heart sank at the thought that things could get worse.

Finally, he opened a drawer in the side table, deposited his wallet, keys, and the bell inside, and closed it quietly.

He'd keep at it, for now, and try to find his way on his own.

The bell was always there if he needed it.

chapter ELEVEN

there's always tomorrow

T he sun was just coming up when Carter awakened. He lay on the couch in the quiet house, listening for the noise that had roused him. He was certain he'd heard something, although in his sleep-slowed mind, he couldn't figure out what it was.

Then he heard it again. A muffled whine . . . or sob. Coming from down the hall.

Thinking maybe one of the kids had had a bad dream, he got up from the couch and followed the sound. As he walked out of the living room, he noticed a dim light coming from the office, and realized that was also where the noises were coming from.

His stockinged feet were silent on the floor as he neared the cracked door. Listening closely, he peered through the small opening, only to see Kenzie sitting at the desk facing the computer screen. She was turned away from him, so he could only see the side of her face, but as she sniffed and wiped a hand across her cheek, he realized she was crying.

"Kenzie?" He pushed the door open and entered the room. "What's wrong?"

Kenzie spun around in surprise and jumped to her feet. "I didn't hear you there."

"Sorry, I didn't mean to scare you." Carter took a step toward her, but stopped short at the look of misery on her face. "What is it?"

Kenzie's face hardened, but the tears continued to roll down her cheeks. Carter tried to look around her at the computer screen to see what she was doing, but he couldn't quite make it out.

"I couldn't sleep," she said, her voice raspy. "I came down here and thought I'd get a little work done. I found an e-mail from our car insurance company. You know how we have it set up for automatic payments from our credit card, then I pay the card off every month?"

Carter felt his stomach tighten. He didn't like where this was going.

"Well, apparently this month's payment was rejected," Kenzie continued, her voice not accusatory, but kind of empty. "I thought it must be some kind of mistake, so I logged on to our Visa account. The card is maxed out, Carter."

Carter swallowed thickly. "It's really not that big a deal—"

Kenzie continued as if he hadn't spoken, her eyes still bright with tears. "So, just on a hunch, I checked our other cards. Can you guess what I found?"

"Kenzie—"

"A little over three-thousand dollars, Carter," she said. "*Three-thousand dollars* in less than a week."

Carter cleared his throat. "Well, I had to pay Lester for fuel . . . and then there was the rental car . . ."

"We worked so hard to pay those off." Kenzie shook her head as if dazed, her voice quiet and lifeless. "After we had to have the roof replaced. Don't you remember? We paid all that interest, and once we got out from under that debt, we decided *together* that we'd keep our credit limits low and pay the cards off every month. And that we'd decide *together* before using them for any major purchases.

"Kenzie, I'll take care of it."

"How, Carter?" she asked, anger beginning to tint her voice. "We barely make enough between us to pay the mortgage and our regular bills. How are we going to find another three thousand dollars?"

Carter ran a hand through his hair in frustration. "I'll find a way. You don't have to worry about it."

"Don't tell me not to worry about it!" Kenzie shouted. She clenched her eyes shut, taking a breath to calm herself. "This affects *both* of us, Carter. Those cards are *ours*. The debt is *ours*. You can't just tell me to not worry about it."

Carter felt his eyes narrow. "And *I'm* telling *you* I'll take care of it. I caused the problem and I'll fix it."

Kenzie collapsed back into her chair. "You just don't get it, do you?" At his blank look, she continued, "We used to be a team. We used to be partners. We're supposed to face things like this together. I've said it over and over again but you never hear me."

Carter collapsed onto a chair. "I just wanted you to have a special night . . . to have some nice things."

"Stop. Please stop, Carter," Kenzie rubbed her eyes. "I don't know how many times I need to say it. I don't need *things*. I just need *you*. I need *us*." She turned to the computer screen, closing windows and shutting everything down. "I have to get to the bank when it opens," she said. "I'm going to try and figure out what to do about the insurance payment."

"I can help," Carter offered.

"I think it would be better if you stayed here," Kenzie countered. "The kids will be up soon." She hesitated, not meeting his eyes. "And I think it might be better if you stayed at Noah's for a little while."

"Kenzie, no," Carter murmured, a wave of panic washing through him.

"I just need some time," she said quietly. "We both need some time, I think, to cool off and get our heads straight."

"Kenzie, don't do this."

"I'm not doing anything, Carter," she said firmly, her hurt, brown gaze meeting his. "I'm asking you to give me some time. Please."

Carter stared at her for a moment before nodding slowly. "Okay."

Kenzie gathered up some papers and walked out of the office. A few minutes later, Carter heard the sound of the front door closing, followed by the rumble of the minivan's engine as Kenzie pulled out of the driveway. He walked over and sat down behind the desk, dropping his elbows to its surface and his face to his palms.

How had this happened? He had such grand plans, and the best of intentions, but—like an idiot—he didn't think it through. He never considered that his spending might actually put a financial hardship on his family. Over the past few years, money hadn't really been an issue for him, but now he kicked himself for not thinking about the consequences of his actions.

He owned a little start-up newspaper in a tiny town. His wife was a school teacher. They had two kids. And it never occurred to him that spending a thousand dollars on a new suit might not be the best idea?

Idiot.

Carter tugged at his hair. He couldn't blame Kenzie for being angry and upset, but he was also starting to feel more than a little frustrated. He really didn't have a clue what was going on— although with every passing moment he was starting to get a better idea—and he was getting tired of paying for mistakes that someone else had made. The *other* Carter. The one who he was beginning to think didn't even deserve Kenzie . . . or this life.

At the same time, he felt a niggling sense of guilt. Because the fact was, the *other* Carter *was* him. The *him* he would have been if he'd made the choices *that* Carter had made. Sure, he could judge that Carter now, from where he stood as an outsider looking in, but in reality he knew he was judging himself. He was getting a glimpse of who he would have been had he made different choices in the past, and to be completely honest, he wasn't too happy with what he saw.

He had no idea what to do about it, though, and he was beginning to think it was time to ask for help.

Carter stood abruptly and walked back into the living room. The sun was up and he could hear the kids moving around upstairs. He went to the side table and pulled the drawer open. He took out his wallet and keys, shifting some papers around as he searched for the little silver bell.

It was gone.

"Oh no," he muttered, pulling everything out of the drawer and setting it on the floor. He even removed the drawer, shaking it upside down before getting down on his knees to search under the table and sofa.

Where was it?

"No, no, no . . ." he chanted, sitting on the floor with his back against the sofa, his knees bent and his head cradled in his arms. "What the hell am I going to do now?"

"Daddy?" A little voice drew him from his agonized thoughts. He looked up to see Brady standing in front of him, his little face red and tear-stained.

The bell forgotten for the moment, Carter reached for his son. "Brady? What's wrong, buddy?"

The little boy's lip trembled. "I'm sorry, Daddy. I did something bad."

Carter ran his hand over the boy's sweat-dampened hair. "It can't be that bad, Brady. Why don't you tell me what happened?"

Brady's head fell forward, his eyes focused on his bare toes. "I, uh, I took your bell."

"You took it?"

"I was looking for my Hot Wheels fire truck and I saw it in the drawer," Brady said in a rush of words. "I'm sorry, Daddy."

Carter felt a surge of relief. "Well, just give it back, buddy. It's okay." He held out his hand and Brady slowly lifted a chubby fist and dropped the bell into Carter's outstretched palm. A curious thought popped into Carter's mind. "Brady, how did you know it was mine?"

Brady swallowed nervously before whispering, "The angel told me."

Carter chilled slightly. "Angel? Do you mean . . . Did you . . . Brady, did you ring the bell?"

Brady nodded, his lip trembling.

"And you saw . . . Henry?"

Brady nodded again.

"Did you talk to him?"

Brady's mouth curved in a slight smile. "He said I shouldn't have taken the bell, but he said you'd forgive me if I said I was sorry."

"What else did he say? Did he say anything else about me?"

Brady bit his lip as he thought. "He told me to tell you, 'That's two.' "

118

That's two. Carter had lost one of his chances to summon Henry for help. He felt a surge of frustration that he'd been held accountable for Brady ringing the bell, but just as quickly, he had to concede that it was his own fault for not keeping the bell on him. He realized his son was watching him warily, most likely still wondering if he was going to get in trouble. Carter smiled and pulled him onto his lap.

"Brady, why did you say that Henry was an angel?"

Brady snuggled into his father's chest. "'Cause of his wings."

"He had wings?"

"Yeah," Brady breathed. "Big white ones." He waved his hands in a big sweeping arc to emphasize his words. "He said most people can't see them, but kids see better than grownups sometimes."

Carter chuckled. "I guess that's true. Did he say anything else?"

Brady nodded against Carter's chest. "I didn't understand it, though."

"What did he say?"

Brady sat up and stared at Carter, his brow creasing as he concentrated. "He said, 'Tell your daddy he has to listen carefully, but not just with his ears. He has to listen with his heart.' That doesn't make sense, does it, Daddy? How can you listen with your heart?"

Carter pulled his son close, pressing a kiss to the top of his head. "I'll have to think about that one, buddy," he said.

And he did. As he got the kids dressed and ready for the day . . . as he fed them breakfast . . . as he packed a bag to take to Noah's . . . and as he passed before Kenzie's sad eyes on his way out the door. She told him she'd managed to get the insurance paid for this month, but they'd have to figure out the credit card problem over the next few days.

Carter had nodded and told her once again that he was sorry.

He knew it wasn't that simple.

However, he was also beginning to realize that maybe it wasn't as *complicated* as he thought. Henry had told him to listen. It was something he really hadn't done much of since he'd arrived in this rather strange life. He thought he knew what Kenzie wanted—what she *needed*—but he never really listened when she told him herself.

What's important to me doesn't even matter to you.

We used to be a team. We used to be partners.

We're supposed to face things like this together.

I've said it over and over again but you never hear me.

I don't need things. I just need you. I need us.

Could it be that all Kenzie wanted was for him to be *with* her? To *listen* to her? To support and encourage her? Could it really be that simple?

Carter had been so busy trying to show Kenzie that she was important to him by giving her *things*, that he didn't even think about just giving her *himself*.

Maybe it was time to try a different tact. Maybe it was time to step back and look at things through Kenzie's eyes.

He could do it.

As he drove to Noah's house, he made a promise to himself. The *other* Carter may have taken his wife and family for granted, but *he* would not. He was going to do whatever it took to make Kenzie realize that he did respect and support her. She would know without a shadow of a doubt that he loved her and the kids . . . and that they were more important to him than any job or missed opportunity.

He would find a way to fix the problem he'd created with the credit card—he felt he owed Kenzie that much. He'd make sure she took the writing class that was so important to her. And he'd find little ways—*inexpensive* ways—to show her how much he cared.

He'd screwed up, but Carter Reed was a man who learned from his mistakes. And there was no way in hell he was losing Kenzie again.

Chapter TWELVE

auld lang syne

C arter spent New Year's Eve sitting on Noah's couch, eating leftover Chinese food, and watching the celebration in Times Square on TV. Noah and Lydia had tried to lure him out to the celebration at *The Mill*, but he'd declined. After spending the day with Kenzie and the kids, he'd returned to Noah's alone.

He sighed as the crowd in Times Square celebrated, but refused to give in to despair.

He was making progress. It was slow. But it was progress.

It started the day he left home. After checking in with Sandi, he'd gone by the bank and spent some time trying to come up with a way to deal with the credit card problem he'd caused. It was no big surprise—although he wished he'd realized it sooner—that he and Kenzie were not rolling in the dough. Between the two of them, they managed to pay their bills and really had very little debt, other than a car payment and the credit cards—the balance of which Carter had managed to more than double with his two-day spending frenzy.

Carter vowed at that moment not to wallow in his mistakes. Instead, he went back to the house in the guise of having forgotten something, and searched through his dresser drawers for a couple of items he was certain he would still have, regardless of the reality he might find himself in.

When his hand closed on the velvet box tucked under his rolled-up socks, Carter breathed a sigh of relief as he recognized it immediately. Before she died, his grandmother had given him the box, telling him to use the contents however he saw fit. He'd always kept it. Even in his other life the box was always tucked deep in his duffle bag. He opened the box, categorizing the items inside quickly. Flipping it shut, he slid it into his coat pocket. He'd have to decide later what he would keep, and what he would sell.

Carter had left the house and gone straight to the office. The paper would go to print the next day, so he had to go over the layout and make sure everything was ready on time. The morning passed in a blur of e-mails and phone calls, as well as frantic knocks on his office door by his assistant editor, Ben Garza. It had been a while since he'd worked on a print publication, so he was grateful for the young man's knowledge and enthusiasm.

During a lull in activity, Carter pulled the box from his pocket and studied the items nestled against the black velvet. Two sets of gold cufflinks winked back at him. One pair was oval-shaped with lapis set in the gold, a thin gold band crossing

123

over the blue stone. The others were jade, slightly smaller, with a twisted gold border. Both dated back to the early twentieth century and Carter knew collectors would go crazy over them. Over the years he'd had them appraised, and there was one antique dealer in Seattle who had called him every few years wondering if he'd be willing to sell.

He was now.

The pocket watch was older—dating back to the Civil War. It had been his great-grandfather's, and Carter really hoped it wouldn't be necessary to sell it, as well. Of all the items in the box, it held the most sentimental value. One of his earliest memories was sitting on his grandfather's lap and watching him carefully wind the old watch.

"Time's the only thing you can never get enough of," he'd told young Carter. "So it's best to use it wisely."

It was a lesson Carter was still learning.

With a little googling, Carter managed to track down the antique dealer he was looking for. Of course, the man had no idea who Carter was, but when Carter described the items in his possession—and subsequently e-mailed pictures of all of them—the dealer had been very interested.

The next day, with the paper put to bed, Carter worked with Sandi to assign the day's stories, then took off for the three-hour trip to Seattle. He spent the time in the car thinking about what he'd learned about Kenzie so far.

She'd become a teacher, but the writing seminar proved that she hadn't given up on her dream of writing. It had been put on the back burner for a while—a long while, apparently. From what Noah had told him, and what he'd gleaned from Kenzie herself, Carter hadn't done much to encourage her to pursue that dream.

Carter planned to change that. He knew first-hand the extent of Kenzie's talent and he understood that she had what it took to be an amazing author. She just had to believe it herself, know that *he* believed it, and have the opportunity to go after it.

It was obvious his alter ego had dwelled on the missed opportunities that came with giving up the internship in New York. Carter, however, knew that what he'd given up was nothing compared to what he'd gained in this alternate reality.

If hindsight was 20/20, what Carter had was even clearer—maybe super-magnification or x-ray vision.

Sure, his career had been rewarding, to a certain extent, but tracking war and famine had already begun to drain him . . . harden him. And even a cushy network news spot didn't compare to his newfound family.

He'd choose Kenzie in a second.

He just had to convince her of that, undo a decade of resentment and regret, and show her that he really did appreciate and love the life that he had now.

Which led to what was the biggest challenge for him—remembering that he and Kenzie were *partners*. Carter had lived on his own for so long it was difficult for him to remember that he and

Kenzie needed to make decisions together. It chafed a little, if he were to be completely honest. To have to run things by someone else smacked a little of asking permission.

But he knew from watching his own parents that it was essential for any marriage to work. It was something he needed to get used to. And he knew he would do it. He'd do whatever it took.

As the Seattle skyline appeared on the horizon, Carter felt a wave of hope rush through him. He may not have known all the details of what led Kenzie and the *other* Carter to this point, but it didn't matter.

It was about moving forward now. And Carter had a plan.

He met with the antique dealer, and after some fierce negotiations, said goodbye to his grandfather's cufflinks and hello to enough cash to pay off the credit cards, plus a little extra. Carter drove home with a smile on his face and a nice check in his pocket.

He'd been able to keep the pocket watch, although he would have parted with it in a second if he needed to. He was quickly learning that he'd do about anything if he needed to—anything that could help fix things with Kenzie and get him back with his family.

What were a set of cufflinks compared to that?

Carter didn't get back to Woodlawn until after dark and knew he'd have to wait until the next day to see Kenzie. He'd shared a late dinner with Noah and Lydia and slept comfortably for the first time since he'd gotten to Woodlawn, even though he was still on a couch.

The next morning, he wiped sweaty palms on his jeans as he stood in his driveway, psyching himself to knock on the front door.

"Got a minute?" he asked Kenzie when she pulled it open, eyeing him hesitantly. "I'd like to talk to you about something."

Kenzie nodded and stepped back from the door. "Would you like something to drink?"

It was something you'd ask a guest. Carter didn't like feeling like a guest. He wanted this to be his home.

"No, thank you," he said politely, hiding his reaction to Kenzie's offer. "Maybe we could sit down?"

He followed her into the living room and sat on the sofa, trying not to frown when she settled on a chair across from him, rather than next to him.

"Where are the kids?" he asked.

"Your mom took them to the indoor play park," she replied. "You know how she loves to spoil them."

They exchanged small smiles and the air thickened with tension.

"So," Carter began, breaking the silence. "I know that we're supposed to make financial decisions together, but I did feel like I needed to deal with the credit card situation, since I'm the one that caused it."

Kenzie blinked in surprise, obviously not expecting him to say that. Carter handed her a sheet of paper with a smile.

Kenzie looked down at the statement from the bank. "I . . . I don't understand. It's paid off?"

Carter nodded, leaning forward to rest his arms on his knees. "They all are. Except for the house and the minivan we are now debt free. And there's enough for that writing class, too."

"But . . . but how?"

Carter shrugged. "I sold my grandfather's cufflinks."

Kenzie gasped. "Carter, you didn't! You love those!"

Carter tilted his head, smiling softly. "I love you more."

"But . . ." Her face flushed as she looked down at the credit card statement again. "Oh, Carter . . . we could have found another way."

"There wasn't another way, Kenzie. You know that."

"I just hate that you had to do it."

"I don't." At her surprised look, Carter added, "They're just things, Kenzie. I don't need *things*. I need *you*. I need *us*." He smiled at the recognition in her eyes when she realized he was using her words. He crossed over to her and dropped to his knees, taking her hands in his. He rubbed his thumbs over her soft skin, gathering his words.

"I know things haven't been right between us for a while," he said earnestly. "To be perfectly honest, I don't completely understand where we went wrong."

Kenzie started to speak, but Carter held up a hand to silence her. "Please, just let me say this?" She nodded and he continued. "Anyway, it doesn't matter, really. I don't want to rehash the past. I want us to start fresh, right now. I want us to get to know each other again . . . to fall in love again. I'm just asking for a chance to build a new life with you, Kenzie. With you and the kids. It's all that matters to me now.

"I know what it's like to live without you," he said, his voice catching when he saw tears begin to glisten in Kenzie's eyes. "That's not a life I want."

Kenzie swallowed thickly. "Me neither."

Carter felt a surge of hope. "Okay, then give us a chance," he said in a rush. "I'm not talking about me coming home, not just yet. I'm talking about us spending time together. I'm asking for you to give us another chance. Give me another chance. Don't give up on us just yet, Kenzie. Can you do that? Just . . . give us some time?"

She reached out to touch his hair, tears trickling down her cheeks. "Yes."

A sunny smile split Carter's face and he leaned forward to kiss her softly . . . chastely. "Okay, then," he said, using his thumbs to brush the tears from her face. "I, uh, I should go, but maybe I could come by tomorrow? We could take the kids to the beach if the weather's not too bad."

Kenzie's face lit up. "That would be really great." She hesitated before asking, "Are you going out with the guys tomorrow night for New Year's?"

"The guys?"

"Yeah? Your friends?"

"Why would I spend New Year's Eve with them?"

Kenzie's brow creased in confusion. "You always spend it with them."

"I do?"

"Carter, are you okay?" Kenzie finally asked. "I mean, not that I'm complaining, but you're acting kind of . . . weird."

Carter missed the question, because something finally clicked. "Kenzie, was I with the guys on Christmas Eve?"

Kenzie's face blanched. "I thought we weren't going to talk about the past."

"I was, wasn't I," he said half to himself. "How much time do I spend going out drinking with the guys?"

Kenzie shrugged. "You need the time away to relax," she replied, obviously quoting an often-heard statement.

"I am *such* a jerk," Carter muttered.

"Carter?" Kenzie was looking at him with concern in her eyes. "What's the matter with you?"

"Good question," he grumbled, his head sagging forward for a moment before he looked back up at her. "Look, Kenzie. I'm done with all of that. I don't need *time away to relax*." He used air quotes to accentuate his contempt for the phrase. "I'm here for you and the kids. All in. We'll hang out tomorrow and if you want to go out for New Year's Eve, I'll take you."

Kenzie frowned. "I'm not really feeling up to it, to be honest."

Carter smirked. "Well, me neither, to be honest. So we'll have a good day and an early night. How does that sound?"

Kenzie smiled. "It sounds perfect. Then, you'll be here for football, right?"

Carter didn't miss a beat. His family had always spent New Year's Day in front of the TV watching bowl game after bowl game. It was something he'd come to miss since he'd left Woodlawn.

"Of course, what time?"

"Oh, whenever. I'll be up early cooking," Kenzie replied.

"I'll come by to help."

"Really?" She laughed. "You want to help cook?"

Carter grinned. "Well, maybe not *cook*, but I can chop and stir with the best of them."

Kenzie stared at him for a moment, then she shook her head slowly. "I can't put my finger on it," she said. "But there's something different about you, isn't there?"

Carter stood, running his hand through his hair. "Yeah, there is."

"What happened?"

Carter reached down to pull Kenzie to her feet, wrapping her in a gentle hug. "I've been given a another chance," he said quietly into her hair, "and I'm going to make the most of it."

Kannawack Beach was a local spot that the tourists eschewed, due to its lack of restaurants and tacky shops hawking flip flops, t-shirts, and cheap sunglasses. Like most of Washington's beaches it was more rocky than sandy, with icy white-capped waves and piles of driftwood and drying bull-whip kelp scattered along the shoreline.

It was cold on the coast in December, and the kids were bundled up in hats and boots. Still, Kenzie had to remind them repeatedly to stay out of the water.

They couldn't resist running up to the lapping waves, and then squealing as they darted back to avoid the rushing water . . . their rubber boots flapping against the sand.

Carter spread out a thick blanket, securing the corners with a cooler and a couple of folding chairs. Kenzie sat next to him as they watched the kids whirl around in circles, holding pieces of the long, whip-like kelp so it twisted around them when they suddenly stopped.

"This is nice," Kenzie said as she wrapped her coat around her and snuggled into one of the chairs.

"It's freezing!" Carter countered, blowing into his hands. "But, yeah. It's nice."

He smiled and Kenzie returned the gesture.

Brady ran up, face red and breath puffing, Peyton dragged behind him.

"Daddy, can we build a sand castle?" he asked.

Carter winced. "I'm afraid this sand isn't great for castles," he replied, letting the damp stuff run through his fingers. "It's not sticky enough. But we could do something better."

"What's better than sand castles?" Peyton asked doubtfully.

Carter grinned. "Let me show you." He rummaged through the duffle bag and pulled a packet from between the towels. It took a few folds and snaps, but before long, he held up the brightly colored plastic and string with a triumphant smile.

"A kite!" Peyton squealed, jumping up and down.

"Can I fly it?" Brady asked, the excitement catching.

"No, me!" Peyton shouted.

"Me!"

"You'll both fly it," Carter said, getting to his feet. "But you're going to take turns."

It was a perfect day for kite flying, a brisk wind steadily whipping along the beach. They ran back and forth, the kids shrieking with delight and the kite heading steadily up, before diving down in an air pocket. It was purple and shaped like a jellyfish, long streamers dangling down below it.

"Hold it tight," he told Peyton as he transferred the spool of string into her hands.

"I've got it, Daddy."

"Yeah, you do."

He left them to it, with Brady hovering protectively over Peyton and the string, and collapsed onto the blanket next to Kenzie.

"I think the kite's a hit," she said, sipping hot tea from a thermos. She offered it to him and he took a drink. "Thanks for thinking of it."

He shrugged, suddenly embarrassed. Should he be thanked for doing something that a dad's *supposed* to do?

133

"Happy to," he said quietly, handing her back the thermos.

They ate sandwiches and chips and built a little fire to roast marshmallows. By the time the sun went down, the kids were stuffed and sleepy-eyed. Kenzie carried Peyton back to the car while Carter carried Brady. He left her to latch the car seats while he returned for the cooler and chairs.

The car was quiet as they drove home, but now and then, he could feel Kenzie watching him. He glanced at her and she smiled.

"What is it?" he asked.

She shrugged. "Nothing, it's just—" She looked out the window on a sigh.

"Just what?"

Kenzie turned back to him and leaned her head on the back of her seat. She smiled softly. "Today was great. Really great. I haven't seen the kids so happy in a long time."

He smiled. "They had a good time."

"Yeah."

"What about you?" he asked. "Did you have a good time?"

She bit her lip and reached across the center console to take his hand, interlacing their fingers. "Yeah, I did."

They held hands the rest of the way home, and carried the sleeping kids up to bed. Carter paused on his way out the front door and ran a hand through his hair.

"Thanks," he said. "For today. For giving me a chance."

Kenzie smiled softly and nodded. "You're welcome." She took a step toward him and hesitated for just a second before popping up on her toes to kiss him on the cheek.

"See you tomorrow?" she asked.

Carter touched his cheek and he felt it all the way to his toes. "Wouldn't miss it."

That kiss lingered on his skin as he drove back to Noah and Lydia's. And by the time the ball dropped, he was already asleep on their couch, a smile on his face.

CHAPTER THIRTEEN

do you know what i know?

C arter was up with the sun on New Year's Day. He was so excited about how well things had gone with Kenzie that he just couldn't stay in bed.

Or . . . on the couch, as the case may be.

So, he was up early, quietly folding his blankets and making coffee for Noah and Lydia. His sister stumbled into the kitchen shortly after seven, her eyes bleary and her hands reaching desperately for the coffee pot. Carter chuckled lightly and poured her a cup. Lydia was never one to sleep in. Even when hungover, she rarely stayed in bed past eight.

"Noah still sleeping?" Carter asked, sipping his coffee and pushing a bag of bagels toward Lydia. She frowned and pushed them back, turning to search for a bottle of aspirin in the cabinet.

"Yeah," she said on a yawn, popping the aspirin dry and chasing it with a gulp of coffee. "You should have come with us last night. We had a blast. Macon and Vi were there, and you remember that guy Tyler Deacon from high school?" At Carter's nod she continued. "He was back in town visiting, and Macon caught him making out in the coat closet with one of the waiters."

Carter laughed. "No way."

"Way," Lydia confirmed, sitting back down at the table. "I think the waiter got fired, but he went home with Tyler, so I guess it's all good."

"Sounds like a great time," Carter said with a grin.

Lydia eyed him closely. "You really stayed in last night?"

Carter nodded. "Yeah, I was pretty beat after chasing the kids up and down Kannawack Beach all day." At Lydia's silent perusal, he asked, "What?"

She shook her head slightly. "Nothing . . . it's just . . . you're usually not one to turn down a party."

Carter grimaced. "Yeah, so I gather."

"What's that supposed to mean?" Lydia looked at him in confusion.

"Nothing. I've just decided to make some changes, that's all."

Lydia continued to stare at him, her eyes narrowing. Carter shifted uncomfortably, swirling the cooling coffee in his cup. His sister had always had a kind of sixth sense about people—an insight that was at times downright eerie. He felt like she was looking into his soul at that moment.

"What's going on with you, Carter?" she asked.

Carter laughed. "You wouldn't believe me if I told you."

Lydia propped her chin on her fists, her gaze unwavering. "Try me."

Carter's smile fell as he considered Lydia's words. What did he really have to lose?

"I'm not the Carter you know," he said finally.

"What do you mean?"

Carter took a deep breath. "I mean, this . . ." He waved his hands to indicate his surroundings. ". . . all of this . . . this *world*. It's not mine. I came from another world . . . another reality."

"Come on, Carter," she snorted.

"I'm serious."

"Like you were serious when we were kids and you'd tell me I was adopted?" she asked. "Or when you convinced me to sleep outside because you could see the future and the house was going to catch fire? Or when—"

"Okay, okay, I get the point," he said, holding up his hands. "But this is different, Lyd. I swear." He reached across the table and grabbed her wrist. "Please, Lyd."

She chewed on her lip for a moment, then nodded ever-so-slightly, and he took a deep breath and proceeded to tell her about the events that led up to his arrival on her couch on Christmas morning. To his surprise, she said nothing while he talked. She didn't interrupt or comment. She just listened.

When he finished, he looked her in the eyes, waiting for her reaction.

"So," she said, tugging on her ear as she often did when thinking deeply about something, "you're saying in your world you never asked Kenzie to marry you?"

"Nope."

"And you guys broke up. You never saw each other again?"

"Not until Christmas Eve when I saw her at the party."

Lydia took a sip of coffee, frowning absently at the cold, bitter liquid. "And that's why you're so different. Why you're so determined to fix things with Kenzie."

Carter nodded. "It sounds crazy, I know."

Lydia chuckled. "Yeah. That's putting it mildly. It's like an episode of *The Twilight Zone*."

"I know. And yet you haven't run out of the room screaming."

She shot him a level look. "I rarely scream."

Carter snorted. "And you don't think I'm crazy?"

"Oh, you're definitely crazy," she said, and he smacked her in the arm.

"Be serious." He met his sister's gaze. "What do you think?"

Lydia shrugged. "I don't know. Something's definitely happened to you . . . and I've never known you to lie to me—I mean, about anything important, anyway. Crazy things happen in the world all the time—so I guess who am I to say what's possible and what isn't?"

Suddenly overcome with emotion, Carter shot to his feet and yanked Lydia up into a tight hug. "Thanks."

She wrapped her arms around her brother and gave him a squeeze. "No problem," she replied. "But, Carter?"

"Yeah?"

"I wouldn't mention this to anyone else," she suggested. "I'd hate to only see you during visiting hours at the asylum."

Carter laughed humorlessly. "Yeah. The thought did cross my mind."

"So what are you going to do now?" she asked.

"Win Kenzie back."

"You make it sound so simple," she said.

Carter released her and returned to his seat. "Well, I have some help now, right?"

Lydia grinned. "You know I'll do whatever I can."

Carter showed up on Kenzie's doorstep just after ten o'clock, clutching a bouquet of brightly colored daisies and a case of beer from the corner grocery store. Kenzie had blushed at the offering, but seemed to like the flowers even more than the roses he'd given her on their disastrous night out.

She'd quickly put him to work chopping vegetables for a thick beef stew and Carter enjoyed the quiet camaraderie as they worked, the kids coloring at the breakfast bar. Brady was uncharacteristically quiet, and Carter found himself watching the boy in concern.

"Brady," he asked finally, "you feeling okay, buddy?"

His son shrugged. Kenzie leaned across the breakfast bar to press her cheek to his forehead.

"You don't have a fever," she murmured. "Does your tummy hurt?"

He shook his head, scratching his crayon across the page, covering it in thick black lines.

"What's wrong, Brady?" Carter asked, fear and concern twisting in his stomach.

The little boy looked up from his picture, his eyes glistening with tears. "Are you getting a divorce?" he asked.

"What's a divorce?" Peyton piped up.

Carter turned panicked eyes to Kenzie, who in turn swept Peyton up into her arms. "Hey, let's go see if we can find the football platters in the garage. Can you come help Mommy?"

Sufficiently distracted, Peyton nodded, wiggling out of Kenzie's grip and running toward the garage.

Which left Carter to deal with Brady's question.

"Why would you ask that, buddy?" Carter sat down next to Brady, reaching out to push the hair back from his forehead.

"Because you don't sleep here anymore," he said through tearful hiccups. "Tanner's daddy stopped sleeping at his house and now his mommy and daddy are divorced and Tanner only sees his daddy on the weekends. And not even *all* the weekends. Only *some* of them."

Carter took a deep breath and pulled the crying little boy into his lap. "Shh . . ." he murmured,

141

rubbing Brady's back gently. When the worst of the sobbing had subsided, Carter turned his son slightly so he could look him in the eye.

"Let me ask you something, Brady," he said. "Have I ever lied to you?" He held his breath waiting for the answer, hoping he wouldn't regret asking the question.

Brady rubbed his fist under his nose. "No."

Carter smiled. "Well, then you know you can believe me when I tell you that no matter where I sleep, I will always be here for you. You and Peyton and Mommy are the most important people in the world to me."

Brady blinked up at him innocently. "Really?''

"Really," he said firmly. "We spent the whole day together at the beach yesterday, right?"

Brady grinned. "That was fun. I got you so wet!"

Carter ruffled his son's hair. "Yeah, you did . . . and I'll be here all day today, too. And if you ever need me, and I'm not around, you just pick up the phone and call me."

"Even at work?" Brady asked doubtfully.

"Any time," Carter told him.

Brady was silent for a moment. "So you're not going to get a divorce?" he asked hopefully.

Carter hesitated. He wanted to calm his son's fears, but could he promise him that? Sure, things were looking better with Kenzie, and if it were up to him, divorce would be out of the question.

But it wasn't entirely up to him.

"No." Kenzie's quiet voice carried from the doorway. She crossed the room, setting an armful of platters on the counter before sitting next to Carter and Brady. Her eyes were on Carter's when she said simply, "No divorce."

"Really?" Brady and Carter said simultaneously.

Kenzie nodded, her attention focusing on her son. "Mommy and Daddy are just having a time out," she explained, reaching out to touch his cheek. "We haven't been treating each other very nicely, but we want to do better."

Brady looked back and forth between his parents for a moment. "I didn't know grownups got time outs," he said.

"We need them sometimes," Kenzie admitted.

"You should be nice," he admonished, turning to his father.

Kenzie and Carter exchanged a smile. "You're right," Carter replied, "and we're working on it, but you don't have to worry, Brady. We'll both always be close by when you need us."

Brady silently absorbed that, then slid off Carter's lap quickly. "Okay," he said brightly. "Can I go watch SpongeBob now?

Carter was a little stunned by the quick change of topic, but Kenzie took it all in stride. "Peyton's watching Dora," she told him. "But when it's over, you can put SpongeBob on, okay?"

Brady agreed with a smile and ran out of the room.

The rest of the day was relaxed and comfortable, and Carter basked in the feeling of being surrounded by family. His parents were there, as well as Stitch, who took up residence on one of the recliners and only got up to get food or run to the bathroom between plays. Lydia, Noah, Macon, and Violet arrived together, and the house was filled with cheers and boos, and the sound of the children playing.

Carter loved every minute of it.

After everyone left, Carter stayed behind to help Kenzie clean up. Once the leftovers had been packed away and all the dishes were washed, he helped put the kids to bed, then grabbed his coat and headed for the door.

"Carter," Kenzie began nervously as he reached for the doorknob. He had a feeling she was going to invite him to stay, but after a moment, she said instead, "Thank you. For all your help today."

Carter smiled and leaned in to kiss her cheek lightly. He was determined not to push things with Kenzie. He was going to take it slow . . . let her learn to trust him again . . . woo her. He was pretty sure he could still woo with the best of them.

"No problem," he said. "Happy to do it. Good night, Kenzie."

"Night."

Carter walked to his car with a skip in his step, and when he lay down on Noah's sofa, his chest felt full and warm. It felt like hope.

True to her word, Lydia was definitely in Carter's corner over the following weeks. She'd often accompany Carter over to the house, offering to sit with the kids so he and Kenzie could go for a walk or get a cup of coffee.

Twice a week, Carter would leave the paper early so he could pick up the kids and Kenzie could go to her writing class in Manaskat. It took a little schedule-shifting, but with Sandi's help, he managed to work it out, and was able to get caught up when the kids were in bed. Carter was a little surprised at how much he enjoyed the one-on-one time with his children. As he got to know them, he found himself falling even more in love with them. He longed to move back home, but he was determined that it would be Kenzie's decision when that would happen.

He continued to look for little ways to make Kenzie feel special—whether it was bringing her more flowers, or one of the cinnamon rolls from *The Mill* that she loved so much. He'd taken to dropping by the house before work a few days a week to take the kids to school and daycare. It gave Kenzie a little time to relax before heading to work and she really seemed to appreciate the gesture.

One day he picked up a pizza from Chicago Ru's and surprised Kenzie at school. The smile on her face when he showed up at her classroom door warmed Carter's heart. Even though Kenzie only had a half hour for lunch, they'd spent it sitting in his car eating pizza and laughing.

"How's the writing class going?" Carter asked through a mouthful of cheese.

Kenzie blushed and reached out to wipe a smudge of sauce from his cheek. "It's good," she said. "Jackson says I have some real talent."

"He's right."

Kenzie picked at her pizza. "You really think so?"

Carter smiled at her. "I know so. You're an amazing writer."

Kenzie looked away, obviously embarrassed by the praise. "There's, uh, going to be a poetry reading on the last night of class," she said hesitantly, her face reddening even more. "It's no big deal. We're all going to share some of the stuff we've written."

"When?" Carter asked.

"The twenty-seventh," she replied. "It's up in Manaskat, so if you can't make it, I totally understand."

"I'll be there."

She smiled at him. "Are you sure?"

Carter set his pizza down and wiped his hands before tucking her hair behind her ear. "I wouldn't miss it. I'm sure my mom or Lydia will watch the kids."

"That really means a lot to me, Carter. Thank you."

"Well, it's really pretty selfish on my part," he replied, his mouth lifting in a smirk.

"Selfish?"

Carter nodded. "Of course. When you become a rich and famous author, I'll be able to ride on your coattails."

Kenzie laughed, and before she ran back to her classroom through the drizzly rain, she'd thanked him and leaned over to kiss him softly, her fingers tangled in his hair.

Carter thought it might have been the best meal he'd ever had.

Chapter
FOURTEEN
deck the halls

Things were going well.

Really well.

As Carter got ready to head to Manaskat for Kenzie's poetry reading, he had high hopes that things would be even better after that evening.

He'd once again picked the children up from school and daycare, feeding them an early dinner before Lydia came over to stay with them. Kenzie had left right after school again for her last class, although it would mainly be a celebration of sorts, as well as final preparations for the poetry reading.

"Are you okay, Carter?" Lydia asked as she watched him fidget with his tie.

A sheepish grin lit Carter's features. "I guess I'm a little nervous."

Lydia crossed to him, straightening his tie and smoothing the shoulders of his suit jacket. "Relax. You'll do fine. I know it means a lot to Kenzie that you're going to be there. And I have a sneaking suspicion you won't be on our couch much longer." She winked.

Carter smiled. "You think so?"

Lydia patted his cheek lightly. "The past few weeks have been good, right?"

"Yeah," Carter said simply. "They've been really good."

And they had. He and Kenzie had been spending more time together, both with and without the children. After the pizza lunch at school was so well-received, he began bringing Kenzie lunch a couple of times a week. He continued to do whatever he could to help out at home, and although he still slept at Lydia and Noah's, there had been more and more late nights devoted to cuddling in front of the fireplace. He and Kenzie had yet to have sex, but things were definitely heating up—and he was beginning to feel that he was the one holding back, not Kenzie.

Carter realized that to her, sex was probably not that big a deal. They had been married for ten years, after all. But for Carter, it had been ten years *since* he'd slept with Kenzie.

It was a lot of pressure.

He'd started noticing some changes on Kenzie's part, too. She was smiling more, and he'd sometimes find her humming quietly as she worked in the kitchen or folded laundry. She seemed to take pleasure in doing little things for him as well—like making the stuffed French toast that he loved, or fixing a missing button on his favorite shirt. (He'd found he really did like flannel after all. It was pretty damn comfortable.)

There were other changes also—times he'd turn to find Kenzie staring at him with a hot look in her eyes. She'd blush and turn away, but Carter could feel the lingering caress of her gaze. He'd done his own share of staring, of course. Kenzie's body called to him like nothing else. It always had. And with each passing day, he felt the simmering tension and he knew the time was drawing near.

Tonight.

He believed . . . God knew he hoped and *prayed* it would be tonight.

A guy could only take so much.

"Carter?" Lydia's voice jolted him out of his lascivious thoughts. "You still with me?" She laughed, waving a hand in front of his dazed eyes.

Carter smirked and leaned over to kiss his sister's cheek. "Not for long," he said lightly. "I've got to go. Don't want to be late."

He arrived at the little restaurant about half an hour early, smiling when he spotted the minivan parked near the rear entrance. Making his way inside, he scanned the crowded room for Kenzie's familiar face. He was a little surprised at how many people had showed up for the reading, but was also excited for Kenzie. It would make the night even more special for her.

He finally spotted her near the stage with a group of people he assumed were her classmates. He waved when he caught her eye, pointing to the table where he was going to sit. He didn't want to interrupt her or make her nervous, but Kenzie smiled and waved excitedly, practically skipping over to greet him.

"You made it," she said breathlessly.

Carter reached out to tug playfully at the ends of her hair. "I told you I wouldn't miss it."

Kenzie hesitated only briefly before she threw her arms around his neck. "Thanks for coming," she murmured into his chest.

Carter encircled her waist, pulling her closer as he nuzzled her neck.

"I love you. So much," he murmured quietly.

Kenzie pulled back, her eyes sparkling. "I love you, too." She bit her lip shyly. "Look, I was going to ask you this later, but now's as good a time as any."

Carter reached up to stroke her cheek. "What is it?"

Kenzie looked away nervously. "I was thinking maybe it was time for you to come home," she said, her face flushing furiously. "I mean . . . if you want to."

Her eyes dropped to the floor and Carter's heart melted. "There's no place I would rather be," he replied earnestly.

Kenzie's head popped back up and a sunny smile lit her face. "Good," she said, "good . . . that's . . . that's . . ."

"Good," Carter concluded with a wry grin.

Kenzie laughed. "Yeah." She looked over her shoulder. "I have to go sit with my class, but maybe afterward we can have something to eat? Celebrate a little?"

"That would be great," Carter said before leaning in to kiss her softly. He'd intended the kiss to be gentle and chaste, but Kenzie apparently had other ideas. She twisted her fingers into his hair, pulling him close as she deepened the kiss. Carter's hands clutched at her waist, and he swallowed her groans as they mingled with his own. When she finally pulled away they were both breathless and warm.

"I have to go," she panted, before leaning in for another kiss.

"Okay," Carter managed to get out before pulling her close again.

"Good evening, ladies and gentlemen." A man speaking from the stage finally managed to break them apart. Carter grinned as Kenzie blushed prettily, squeezing his hand before returning to her seat across the room.

"It's a very special night here at Riley's," the man continued. "This is the first time we've hosted a poetry reading, and from this turnout, I can tell you it won't be the last."

The room broke out in low chuckles before he continued. "I'd like to introduce you to the man who's made all of this possible, but I know he really needs no introduction. Please welcome, *New York Times* bestselling author, Jackson McKay!"

Loud applause echoed against the walls as a tall, lanky man with a ponytail made his way to the microphone. He nodded at the crowd, obviously used to the adulation. Carter hadn't read any of his books, but knew that McKay was a successful writer. Of course, in Carter's world, Kenzie was even more successful.

Take that, Jackson McKay, he thought with a slight smirk.

"Thank you," McKay said finally. "Thank you for the warm welcome, and for coming out to support these up and coming writers." He waved a hand toward Kenzie's table and the applause began again.

The night was entertaining, for the most part. McKay made a point of saying something about each of the students before they took the stage to read their work. Some of it was quite impressive. Some, not so much.

Carter had to swallow his laughter when a middle-aged man named Tony recited a rather graphic poem heralding the advantages of loving a plus-sized woman. When he actually used the phrase, *more cushion for the pushin'* with longing in his voice, Carter cleared his throat to cover his chuckles. As he gazed around the room, he found several other people in the same predicament.

Finally, it was Kenzie's turn.

"Mackenzie Reed is a rare talent," McKay said with a fond glance toward Kenzie.

It almost seemed . . . *too* fond.

Carter stiffened, his eyes narrowing.

"She came to me at a seminar I taught in Portland a month ago, and I knew hers was a gift that needed nurturing if it was going to flourish." McKay smiled at Kenzie, who blushed under the praise. Carter felt an instinctive tightening of his muscles, a primeval craving to protect what was his.

He knew in that instant that Jackson McKay wanted his wife. He felt a rage unlike any he'd ever felt before rear up inside of him, and he clenched his teeth tightly shut, fearing if he didn't that an actual growl would burst through his lips.

He tore his eyes from McKay, no longer listening to what he was saying. He found Kenzie watching him with concern in her eyes.

Carter took a deep breath. This was an important moment for Kenzie, and he would not ruin it for her. He forced an encouraging smile and began to applaud as McKay called her to the microphone. Carter fought to maintain his composure as McKay hugged Kenzie quickly before leaving the stage.

He'd deal with that guy later.

"Thank you, Jackson," Kenzie said in a quiet voice, clearing her throat nervously. "And thank all of you for coming. This is a poem I call *Light*. It's . . . it's for Carter."

Carter blinked in surprise and sat up a little in his chair, all thoughts of Jackson McKay forgotten as Kenzie unfolded a sheet of paper and began to read.

Our love began long ago . . . in the sunrise of our lives

When everything was bright and new and filled with warm rosy light

We laughed in the heat of our passion and smiles

Two moving as one . . .

Living as one . . .
Loving as one.

Her gaze flashed up briefly to catch his, a small smile lighting her face. Carter smiled back, mesmerized by her.

But all too soon, the light grew dim . . . as shades and shadows fell

A darkness-built wall erected between us, bricks of indifference and complacency

And we were lost

Two moving as two . . .

Living as two . . .

Loving . . .

No . . . not loving.

Just two.

Carter felt a lump in his throat and he could hear Kenzie's voice shaking slightly as well, although she kept her eyes firmly focused on the paper. Her fingers gripped the edges of the sheet and she took a deep breath before continuing.

And yet . . .

The wall, the darkness, was not impenetrable.

A ray of light shown through . . . warm and rosy and glowing.

Light shattered bricks one by one, grinding them to dust.

Until all that was left was the intensity of the light's heated rays

Glistening and shining on my skin . . . sparkling in my eyes.

She looked up, tears streaming down her face as she met Carter's gaze. He was surprised to find his cheeks were damp as well. She smiled triumphantly as she read the last line.

The light was you.

Kenzie stepped down from the stage to hugs from her classmates and resounding applause. Carter continued to clap as he approached her, ignoring the crowd, his eyes focused only on Kenzie. He came to a stop in front of her, reaching out tentatively, then pulling her close.

"My God, Kenz, that was incredible," he murmured in awe.

"You really liked it?" she asked.

Carter released her so he could look in her eyes. "It was beautiful," he said earnestly. "Really, Kenzie. I loved it."

"Told you so," Jackson McKay said with a wide grin, looping his arm over Kenzie's shoulders. She shrugged uncomfortably and his arm slipped off. McKay seemed not to notice and tucked his hand into his pocket instead. "You have real talent, Kenzie," he said. "You get a manuscript completed and I'm going to set up a meeting with my agent."

"Really?" Kenzie's eyes widened.

"Absolutely," he said, placing his hands on her shoulders and effectively blocking Carter out. Carter stood close by her side, his fists clenched. "I believe in you, Mackenzie," McKay said, squeezing her shoulders slightly. Carter's eyes narrowed at the movement of the man's fingers. He really didn't want to ruin this moment for Kenzie, but the guy was crossing a line.

"Thank you, Jackson," Kenzie said quietly before stepping toward Carter and wrapping her arm around his waist. Once again, McKay's arms fell to his sides and Carter fought a smug grin.

"This is my husband, Carter," Kenzie told him. "Carter, meet Jackson McKay."

"Ah, the famous Carter," McKay said with a knowing grin. "Almost let this one get away, did you?" He chuckled, but Carter caught the glint in his eye. The glint of challenge. The glint of warning.

"*Almost* being the key word," Carter said pointedly as he shook the man's hand, a warning of his own in his gaze.

"Well, I need to go mingle," McKay said, ignoring the challenge. "Kenzie, are you going to stay around for drinks?"

She shook her head. "No, Carter and I are going to have something to eat and then head home. Early day tomorrow."

McKay nodded. "Very well. I'll be in touch," he said, turning to walk to the bar.

"That guy's an ass," Carter muttered without thinking.

"Carter." Kenzie rolled her eyes. "He's helped me a lot."

"I'm sure he has."

"What's that supposed to mean?"

Carter took a deep breath. He really didn't want to get into this now. "Nothing. Let's get something to eat."

"No, don't do that, Carter," Kenzie insisted, pulling him over to a quiet table. "If something's bothering you, we need to talk it out."

Carter eyed her carefully. "I don't want to argue here."

"We don't have to argue," she pointed out. "We could discuss it."

Carter chuckled humorlessly. "I don't know about that."

Kenzie smiled. "Try me."

Carter considered it for a moment, then said slowly. "It's McKay. That guy has more on his mind than your writing talent."

Kenzie blinked in surprise. "You can't be serious."

"I saw how he looks at you, Kenzie. He's definitely interested."

Kenzie flushed, her voice trembling slightly. "That's pretty insulting, Carter."

"Insulting?" That was definitely not the response Carter was expecting. "How is that insulting?"

Kenzie glared. "That you'd think Jackson McKay could only be interested in my body. That there's no way he could actually think I'm a talented writer."

"That's not what I said," Carter fought to keep his voice low. "You *are* a talented writer. But that's not why he feels it's necessary to keep touching you."

"For God's sake, Carter," Kenzie groaned. "He's only being friendly."

"That's what they call it now?"

"Carter!"

"No, don't downplay this, Kenzie," Carter said through gritted teeth. "I'm not being ridiculous. That guy wants you and he's made it very clear he's going to go after you."

"Clear to who?" Kenzie asked, mystified.

"To me."

She stared at Carter like he'd grown a third head. "What in the world are you talking about?"

"You didn't hear that little *almost let this one get away* dig?" he asked.

"Really, Carter? That's what all this is about?" Kenzie gaped. "You don't think maybe you're overreacting just a teensy bit?"

"Don't mock me, Kenzie." Carter stood up abruptly. "Look, I don't think this is the place for this conversation. Let's go. We can talk about this at home."

Kenzie bristled slightly. "What if I'm not ready to go?"

Carter's shoulders fell. "Well, so much for discussing without arguing," he muttered.

At that, Kenzie exhaled heavily. "I'm sorry. It's my fault. You didn't want to talk about it and I dragged it out of you."

"I didn't really fight you too hard on it," Carter admitted. "The guy seriously pissed me off."

Kenzie laughed slightly. "Look, I still think you're overreacting . . ." She held up a hand when Carter opened his mouth to argue, ". . . *but* I'm willing to hear you out. You're right, though. This isn't the place.

"Why don't I stay for a bit, say goodbye to my classmates, and pick up some takeout. You can go home and relieve Lydia. When I get there we can eat and really have a *discussion*." She emphasized the word and made Carter smile.

"Sounds good," Carter said before leaning in to kiss her . . . softly at first, but when he saw McKay watching, he couldn't resist making it a little hotter. He left Kenzie dazed and breathless, and walked to his car with a little spring to his step.

He was almost back to Woodlawn when his phone rang.

Recognizing the number, he answered quickly. "Kenzie?"

"Carter, uh, something's happened."

"What is it? Are you okay?" He pulled over to the side of the road quickly. "Is there something wrong with the car?"

"No, the car's fine," she replied. "I'm fine . . . it's just . . ."

"Kenzie, what is it?"

"Remember—I'm fine," she said again firmly. "And Carter, please don't say *I told you so*," she added.

"Kenzie, what's going on? You're scaring me," he said frantically.

"I'm in the ER," she said on a heavy sigh. "I'm okay, but I think I broke my hand."

Carter had flipped a U-turn and was barreling back down the highway before he asked, "How in the world did you break your hand?"

Kenzie hesitated briefly before sighing again and replying, "I punched Jackson McKay in the jaw."

CHAPTER FIFTEEN

where the love light gleams

Carter ran through the doors to the emergency room, waiting impatiently at the check-in desk as a woman with a crying baby paid her co-payment. When the exhausted woman finally turned to find a seat in the crowded waiting room, Carter leaned onto the counter anxiously.

"My wife is here," he told the woman. "Mackenzie Mon—Mackenzie *Reed*," he corrected quickly. "Can you tell me where she is?"

The nurse clicked some keys on her computer. "Ah, yes, Mr. Reed," she said after a moment. "The doctor's just finishing up with your wife. You're welcome to have a seat, or if you'd like to join her—"

Carter didn't let her finish. "I'd like to join her. Please," he added at the woman's raised eyebrow.

The nurse smirked. "Through the doors, second curtain on the right," she said, pointing at a set of swinging doors.

"Thank you," Carter replied before following the woman's instructions. He found Kenzie sitting on a gurney, a petite redhead in scrubs bent over her arm, adjusting a splint. Kenzie looked up as he approached.

"Carter!" she exclaimed cheerfully. "You're here!"

"Kenz, are you okay?" He reached out to touch her, but then pulled back quickly, worried he might hurt her.

"I'm fine!" she waved her good arm, then seemed distracted by the movement, watching closely as her arm waved back and forth.

"Doctor?" Carter turned to the red-haired woman. "What's wrong with her? Did she hit her head?"

The doctor smiled up at him. "I assume you're Mr. Reed?"

"Carter," he corrected.

"Well, Carter, Kenzie here is just fine. She's got what we call a boxer's fracture," the doctor explained. "It's not too bad. No need for a cast. She'll just need to wear this splint for a few weeks to give it time to heal."

"I punched Jackson, Carter," Kenzie interrupted. "I punched him good." She swung her uninjured fist, almost falling off the gurney.

"Yeah." The doctor laughed. "She was in quite a bit of pain when she got here, so I gave her a little something."

Kenzie held her thumb and finger an inch apart, squinting at Carter between them as she whispered, "Li'l something."

163

Carter's mouth lifted in a half-grin. "You feeling okay, Kenz?"

"I feel great!" she exclaimed, blinking widely. "How are you?"

"I'm fine," he replied on a laugh, turning back to the doctor. "When can I take her home?"

The doctor signed a prescription pad, ripped off a slip, and handed it to Carter. "She's all done. You'll want to get that filled before you go home. Once the medication wears off, she might need it."

Carter nodded, tucking the slip in his pocket and thanking the doctor. He reached for Kenzie's arm. "You ready to go home?"

"Yup!" she said cheerfully, hopping to the floor. Her knees buckled and she fell into Carter. He caught her easily.

"Oops." Kenzie giggled.

"I've got you, baby," Carter murmured, helping her out of the curtained area.

"I love it when you call me baby," she whispered back.

Carter kept his arm wrapped tightly around Kenzie's waist as they left the hospital. The nurse at the check-in desk had assured him it would be all right to leave the minivan overnight as long as he returned the next day to get it.

"I can drive home, Carter," Kenzie had protested.

"Kenzie, you broke your hand, remember?"

"Oh, yeah."

He helped Kenzie into the car, reaching across her to buckle the seatbelt. He jumped slightly when he felt her mouth on his neck.

"You smell so good," she said against his skin.

"Thank you."

"Really, Carter," she said earnestly. "You smell *amazingly* good. I could smell you all day."

Carter chuckled. "Well, you can smell me anytime."

He got into the driver's seat and backed out, turning toward home. He glanced over to see Kenzie watching him closely, her eyes slightly glazed.

"You're so hot," she said.

Carter smirked. "You're so high."

"I mean," Kenzie continued, not hearing his comment, "you were hot when I first met you. I mean you were all tall and brooding and intense and handsome. But now . . . now you're even hotter. With the scruff and the shoulders and the— You're like *inferno-hot*."

Kenzie rambled on, her words slurring slightly. "Sometimes I see you, and I just want to climb on . . ."

Her voice trailed off and Carter looked over at her. Kenzie's eyes were closed and she snored lightly.

"Sleep tight, Slugger," he whispered before turning back toward the highway.

Kenzie woke with a start when Carter pulled up in front of the house. He'd stopped at an all-night pharmacy to pick up her prescription, and stuffed the bag into his pocket before rounding the car to help Kenzie out.

"Carter?" she mumbled. "My hand hurts."

"I know, baby. Come on, let's go inside." He led her carefully up to the front door, unlocking and shoving it open with his foot before helping her in. He'd called Lydia from the hospital and knew she'd be sleeping on the couch. Kenzie's wooziness had worn off, but he still supported her as they made their way upstairs and into their room.

"You were right about Jackson. He is an ass," Kenzie said with a wince as she sat down on the bed and leaned back onto the pillows.

Carter stiffened, but tried to at least put on a façade of calm. "What did he do?"

"Tried to kiss me."

"And you punched him?" Carter couldn't keep the proud smirk off his face.

Kenzie shrugged. "He wouldn't take no for an answer."

Carter sat down on the edge of the bed. "You are a formidable woman, Mrs. Reed," he said with a grin.

"Are you mad?" she asked.

"At you? No. At him? There are no words to describe the depths of my fury."

Kenzie grinned. "You're mighty formidable yourself, Mr. Reed."

"Don't you forget it." He reached out to touch her hair. "I'm sorry you're hurt."

"Thanks."

Carter stood up. "Let me help you get ready for bed, and I'll get going." He bent down to untie her shoes.

"Or you could stay," Kenzie offered hesitantly. "It's late, and there's no reason for you to drive all the way over to Noah's."

"I wouldn't want to hurt you," he said, indicating her arm.

"I'll be fine," she replied with a smile. "You sleep on the left anyway."

Carter returned to the task of removing Kenzie's shoes. "Okay, then. If you're sure."

"I'm sure."

He pulled off her jacket and jeans carefully, and tucked her beneath the sheets after giving her a pain pill. He shed his own clothes, crawled in on the other side of the bed, and turned out the light.

"How's your arm?" he asked into the darkness.

"Not too bad . . . kind of numb. It's not what hurts the most anyway."

Carter turned to her, barely making out her profile in the dim light coming through the window. "What do you mean?"

He felt her shrug. "I just feel like an idiot, that's all. I mean, for a writer like Jackson McKay to say I had some talent . . . it was a real ego boost, I'm not going to lie. But to find out that all he wanted was . . . Well, it's a blow, you know?"

Carter reached out to take Kenzie's good hand. "Don't give up because of him, Kenz."

"I don't know . . ."

"I *do* know," he said vehemently. "Kenzie, you do have a gift. You are an amazing and talented writer, and you have it in you to be bigger than Jackson McKay ever was."

"That's really sweet of you to say."

"No, I'm not being sweet," Carter insisted. "I'm telling you the truth, Kenzie. I believe in you. You can do this. Don't let that piece of—" He took a breath. "Don't let him take your dream away from you. Don't let anyone."

Kenzie turned onto her side, resting her injured arm carefully on her hip. Carter could see her eyes shimmering slightly. "You really believe that, don't you?"

"I do."

"Thank you, Carter." He felt her watching him for a moment before she added, "Would you do something for me?"

"Anything."

"Would you come over here and hold me? It's been a long time."

"Too long," Carter agreed, shifting closer to her and sliding his arm carefully under her shoulders. She cuddled closer to him, her leg over his and her injured hand on his heart. He ran his fingers through her hair slowly and pressed a kiss to her head.

"I've missed this," she murmured.

"Me, too."

"Good night, Carter."

"Good night, Kenzie."

Carter moved back home, and back into his bedroom. Kenzie was still hurting, and with her hand in a splint, needed some extra help around the house. She took a couple days off work, but as the pain lessened to more of a dull throb than a sharp stab, she told Carter it was time for her to go back.

"Are you sure you're ready?" Carter asked the night before she was scheduled to return to the classroom. They were lying in bed with Kenzie's back tucked up against Carter's bare chest. His arm encircled her waist as she held his hand against her stomach. "Those fourth-graders can be ruthless," he added.

Kenzie laughed. "I'll be fine. I have an aide to help me out, and my students are wonderful," she said pointedly.

"How's your hand? Do you need a pill?"

He felt Kenzie shake her head under his chin. "No, I took a couple of Ibuprofen and it's fine," she replied. "Don't worry so much."

"I just want to take care of you," he said quietly. "I almost lost you and I don't ever want that to happen again."

"Carter, it's just a little fracture."

"That's not what I'm talking about."

Kenzie was silent for a moment. "I know." She shifted, turning around to face him. The full moon shone through the window and Carter could barely make out her features where her head lay on the pillow next to his.

"It wasn't just you, Carter," she said, her eyes glistening pools in the moonlight. "It wasn't all your fault."

"But I—"

She cut him off. "We were both there, Carter. We *both* did our part to drive a wedge between us." She reached out to stroke his hair gently. "I blamed you."

"For what?"

She laughed. "For everything. For getting married young. For having kids. For living in Woodlawn and not getting my Master's . . . for giving up on writing."

"I didn't make it any easier for you," he pointed out.

"But it was *my* choice," she countered emphatically. "It was easier to blame you than to accept responsibility myself. And instead of talking to you about it, I just kept it all inside, letting the resentment build and turn me into some kind of icy b—." She shook her head. "I was cold. I was *cruel*. I could hardly blame you for wanting to get out of the house."

"That doesn't make it right."

He saw the glint of Kenzie's teeth as she smiled wryly. "No. It doesn't. But it does make it understandable. I pushed you away. I held on to my frustration and took it out on you."

"Kenzie—"

"No . . . no, please, let me say this," she interrupted. "I'm sorry, Carter. I'm sorry for blaming you and for cutting you out. I'm sorry that when you tried to help me out around the house all I could do was criticize. I'm sorry for turning away from you. I'm sorry for—"

Her words were lost as Carter finally leaned over to kiss her. After a moment, he pulled back. "I'm sorry, too," he said. "But I think it's time to be done with apologies."

Kenzie smiled again. "Yeah. I guess so."

They stared at each other in the darkness, the only sounds the ticking of the bedside clock and their quiet breathing.

"You know, I've been thinking," Kenzie whispered.

"About what?"

"Second chances."

Carter took her splinted hand carefully, kissing her fingers. "What about them?"

Kenzie shrugged. "Just that maybe they aren't about fixing mistakes as much as learning from them."

Carter smiled. "I think maybe you're right."

"Carter?"

"Yeah."

"I've really missed you."

"I missed you too, baby."

Kenzie moved closer to him, resting her splint on his hip. "I really love it when you call me baby," she whispered.

"Yeah, you mentioned that," he said with a grin.

Suddenly the air between them changed . . . thickened . . . charged with something Carter couldn't name, but could definitely identify. Kenzie tilted her chin, brushing her lips against his softly before sucking his bottom lip into her mouth, releasing it with a soft pop.

"Kenzie," he whispered, "what about your arm?"

"My arm is fine," she replied, sliding her good hand down between them to stroke his abdomen, lifting his shirt to caress his bare skin.

"Are you sure about this?" he asked, unable to keep from pulling her closer, dipping his chin to kiss her again.

"Carter . . . please . . ." She breathed out between increasingly desperate kisses. "You're not going to make me beg, are you?"

"Perish the thought," Carter muttered on a long moan, giving in . . . giving up . . . giving over to the feelings he'd been fighting for so long. He rolled over carefully, avoiding Kenzie's splint. After only a brief hesitation—more to savor the moment than to question it—he kissed her deeply, pressing her into the pillow as his tongue slid into her warm mouth.

"I love you," he whispered between her lips. "I've wanted this for so long."

"Me, too." She clutched at him with her good hand, pulling him closer. "I love you so much."

He kissed her again, softly then deeply, determined to make it last . . . to make a beautiful new memory for both of them. He gently moved her splinted hand so it rested on the pillow next to her head, then slid his hand down her side slowly, rubbing soft circles with his thumb.

She used to like that.

When she whimpered slightly, he smiled as he realized she still did.

He pulled her night shirt up, shifting to the side so he could slide it over her head. He gasped at the sight of her bare skin, unable to resist leaning down to taste it. Kenzie clutched at his hair, arching upward with a moan and Carter couldn't believe it was real.

"It is," she said, and he realized he'd said that out loud.

She shoved at his shirt, impatient, and he tugged it over his head. With a victorious laugh, she tilted her head and sank her teeth into his bare shoulder.

He let out a very unmanly sound and she giggled.

Carter's eyes narrowed, even though in the dim light Kenzie couldn't see them. "You're enjoying driving me crazy, aren't you?" he accused.

Kenzie giggled again. The sound made Carter want to shout for joy.

"Maybe," she replied saucily.

"Well, two can play at that game," he warned, moving to attack her own neck.

They laughed and whispered in the lingering dark, rediscovering each other with each gentle touch and passionate kiss. It had been ten years since he'd been able to touch her like that, but as they said, it was like riding a bike.

Except much, much better.

Carter watched Kenzie as she came apart in his arms, the splinted hand by her head, the other gripping his hair wildly. He marveled at the feel of her, the taste of her skin, the sound of her heart beating, blood pulsing beneath his fingers. So real and precious he couldn't imagine anything before or after her.

And as they finally joined together, his eyes clenched shut as her warmth enveloped him, Carter knew he had come home.

As he moved—slowly at first, then faster and deeper, feeling Kenzie accepting him, drawing him closer—he believed he'd found heaven.

As he watched her—as they watched each other—eyes locked as they tipped over that precipice between pleasure and pain . . . between love and loss . . . he vowed he'd never leave her again.

And as he collapsed next to her, tucking her into his arms and stroking her back as she drifted off to sleep, he said a silent prayer, thanking God for second chances.

Chapter
SIXTEEN
baby, it's
cold outside

The next morning, the sun was shining, the birds were singing, and the joyous sound of children's laughter filled the air.

Okay, not really.

It was Woodlawn, after all. It was cloudy and raining. The birds were notably absent, probably huddled under a bush somewhere to try and stay dry. As for the children, they were arguing about whether or not SpongeBob could survive in the bathtub.

But for Carter? Yeah, it was all sunshine and rainbows.

"Good morning," he said with a grin as he swept into the kitchen, grabbing Kenzie and bending her over backward before planting a lingering kiss on her lips.

"Eeewww gross!" Brady complained, all thoughts of SpongeBob forgotten as he covered his eyes.

Carter could see him smiling, though, so he kissed Kenzie once more for good measure before setting her back on her feet. She stroked his cheek with a smile and turned back to the bacon. He stood behind her and rested his hands lightly on her hips, his chin on her shoulder.

"Hungry?" she asked.

"Starving," he growled, nuzzling her neck until she giggled. Carter chuckled, squeezing her once more before he released her and walked around to sit by the kids at the breakfast bar. Brady still had his hands on his eyes, so Carter pulled them down playfully.

"All done," he reassured his son.

"Good," Brady replied, rolling his eyes dramatically. Carter ruffled his hair and leaned in to kiss his daughter on the cheek.

"How are you this morning, beautiful?" he asked her.

Peyton smiled prettily. "Fine, Daddy."

"Hey, I have an idea," he said, reaching out to pull her onto his lap, sliding her plate of scrambled eggs and toast over so she could reach it. "How about tonight I pick up a pizza and we have a Candy Land Championship Marathon!"

"Yes!" Brady fist pumped as Peyton bounced excitedly on her father's lap. "I'm gonna win!" the little boy shouted.

"I don't think so," Carter warned. "I am *very* good at Candy Land."

"Daddy?" Peyton placed her palms on Carter's cheeks, turning his face to her. "Can I be pink?"

"Pink?"

176

"The pink gingerbread man," she explained.

Carter nodded between her hands. "Sure, sweetie."

Brady spun around on his barstool. "There is no pink in Candy Land."

"Yes, there is," his sister replied stubbornly.

"Nope," he said, tucking his feet up so he could spin faster. "Only red, blue, green, and yellow!"

"Daddy?" Peyton turned pleading eyes toward him. He looked toward Kenzie for help, but she just shrugged at him and stirred the eggs.

"Uh . . ." Carter floundered slightly, but then got an idea. "I'll stop by the hardware store and pick up some paint and we'll *make* a pink piece," he said, his chest swelling at the awed look on his daughter's face. She stuck her tongue out at Brady, who didn't notice because he was still spinning.

All was good.

"I really need to go," Carter said, his actions belying his words as he pressed Kenzie against the front door, his lips at her neck. He could hear the kids running around upstairs looking for their shoes and coats and was taking the opportunity to say goodbye properly to his wife.

Repeatedly.

"Yeah, you should definitely go," Kenzie replied breathlessly, her fingers sliding into his hair as she tugged his mouth back to hers.

"Early meeting," he murmured into her mouth.

"Uh huh." Kenzie deepened the kiss, her hands dropping down to his hips, pulling him against her.

"*Oh God.* Maybe I could call in sick?" Carter offered, brushing his thumb over her breast. Even through her thick sweater he could feel her respond.

"Mmm . . ."

"We could spend the whole day in bed."

"Mommy, Brady said girls are stupid!" Peyton's outraged screech from the top of the stairs effectively ruined the mood. Still, Carter found himself smiling at the interruption. He backed away from Kenzie after one more quick kiss, just as the two children came down the stairs.

"I did not!" Brady explained, directing his words at his father, obviously hoping another male would support his viewpoint. "I said girls do stupid *things*," he clarified.

"Well, Brady, was that a very kind thing to say?" Carter asked.

Brady crossed his arms over his chest, betrayed by his father's lack of manly backup. "No," he grumbled.

"And it's not really true, is it? I mean, some girls do stupid things sometimes, but boys do, too, right?"

Brady huffed in exasperation. "Right."

"Don't you think a comment like that might hurt your sister's feelings . . . or even Mommy's?" Carter pointed out.

Brady looked up at his mother guiltily. "I didn't mean to."

"I know you didn't." Carter rubbed his son's head. "But maybe you should make it right?"

Brady swallowed thickly. "I'm sorry." He reached over to hug his sister quickly, then his mother. Kenzie dropped to her knees to kiss the little boy's cheek.

"All's forgiven," she said cheerfully. "Now, are we ready for school?"

The family left the house together, Carter managing to steal one more kiss before getting into his car. He watched Kenzie and the kids in the minivan in front of him until they turned left to head to Peyton's daycare as he continued on straight to the paper.

Overall, he was feeling pretty good about things. He might have been new to the whole husband and father gig, but he seemed to be catching on. Carter whistled cheerfully through his teeth as he pulled up in front of the *Weekly*, winking at Sandi as he made his way to the little conference room next to his office for the morning staff meeting. After brainstorming ideas for the next issue with the rest of the staff, Carter and Ben made the initial assignments so Sandi could post them on the white board.

Lunchtime found him daydreaming at his desk, googling ideas for Valentine's Day. Nothing too over the top—he'd learned his lesson about that— but he definitely wanted to do something special for Kenzie. He still had a few weeks, but Carter was excited and didn't want to leave it until the last minute.

They could go to dinner at *The Mill*. The food there was actually pretty good . . . then maybe a drive up the coast to watch the sunset.

Or maybe a picnic? They could go to the beach—or maybe out to the meadow where they used to go when they were teenagers. Carter smiled at the memory of the first time he kissed Kenzie. They'd skipped school with some friends and shared a bottle of Boone's Farm in the meadow as they huddled under heavy blankets. He'd turned to her, extending his arm to offer her half of his blanket. When she'd snuggled next to him, he couldn't resist leaning down to kiss her softly.

She'd smiled up at him, and even then he knew his heart was lost.

The meadow was definitely a good idea. No Boone's Farm, though. He could afford a halfway decent bottle of champagne—and maybe a tent and a portable heater to keep warm. He'd have to work on that.

Unfortunately, work kept him busy for the rest of the afternoon, giving him little time to fine-tune his plans. He did remember to call ahead to order the pizza before he left the office. Kenzie had a couple of parent conferences after school, and by the time she picked up the kids and made it home, he'd have the table set and the Candy Land game ready.

He was about to walk out the door when a screechy call came across the scanner on Sandi's desk. She reached over to adjust the volume, listening carefully and jotting down a few notes.

"Sounds like a bad accident over on Division Street," she said. "I can call Alex and get him over there."

Carter shook his head. Car accidents usually didn't make the *Weekly*, simply because by the time the paper went to print they were old news. Still, he couldn't ignore it. "No need," he replied. "I have to go that way to head home anyway. I'll check it out."

"You sure?"

"Yeah. It's no problem," Carter assured her. "I'll talk to the cops and get a few pictures. If it's a big deal, I'll call Alex myself."

He double-checked his bag to make sure he had a tape recorder and camera handy, then got in his car and headed toward the accident scene. Traffic was blocked off a short distance away. He could make out the flashing police lights, but not much else in the dimming light. Carter parked at the curb and approached the uniformed deputy at the roadblock. Just as he said hello, his cell phone rang.

Not recognizing the caller's number, he thumbed at the screen. "Excuse me," he said to the deputy, before answering the phone.

"Hello?"

"Carter, it's Stitch."

Carter was surprised to hear his father-in-law's voice and hesitated briefly before replying, "Hi, Stitch. How are you?"

"Carter there's no easy way to say this . . . there's . . . there's been an accident." Stitch's voice trembled slightly, confusing Carter even more.

"Yeah . . . I know. I'm down here to cover it for the paper."

He heard Stitch clear his throat before continuing. "No. You don't understand, son. It's Kenzie."

Carter felt Stitch's words like a punch in the stomach. *It's Kenzie.* He couldn't mean—

"What?" he asked, the word barely making it past his lips.

Stitch sniffed and Carter realized the man was crying. "It's Kenzie, Carter. She's been hurt."

"Oh, God . . . no . . ." Carter murmured, panic beginning to sizzle along his nerve endings. "Is she okay? Where are the kids?" He began to make his way through the road block, ignoring the deputy who called for him to stop. "Stitch, is she okay?" He started to run in the direction of the flashing lights. When he made out the tangled pile of metal that used to be his minivan, an anguished cry tore from his throat.

"Carter . . . Carter!" He heard Stitch calling to him and pressed the phone to his ear. "The kids are okay, but Kenzie . . ." His voice broke. "I'm with her now at the hospital. You need to get over here, Carter."

He turned to run back to his car, but a strong hand gripped his elbow. He turned to see Macon Bridges looking down at him with compassion in his eyes.

"I was passing by and saw what happened," he explained. "Let me take you to the hospital, Carter. You shouldn't be driving."

Carter couldn't reply. He just nodded jerkily and followed Macon to his truck. It was only a few blocks to the hospital and Macon made it in record time. He pulled up in front of the emergency entrance and Carter jumped out before the truck rolled to a stop, racing through the sliding doors. He spotted Stitch immediately, standing next to the reception desk.

"How is she?" Carter asked frantically.

Stitch shook his head. "I don't know. The doctors are with her now."

"What about the kids?"

"They're fine," he replied. "I was just in there with them. They're pretty shaken up, but they'll be okay. Just some cuts and scrapes. Come on, I'll take you back."

He led Carter through a door into an examining area and Carter breathed a sigh of relief when he saw Brady and Peyton sitting on a couple of chairs sucking on lollipops. Brady had a Band-Aid on his forehead, and Peyton's right hand was wrapped in gauze, but other than that, they looked uninjured. He rushed over to pull them both in a tight hug.

"Are you guys okay?" he asked, running his hands over their heads and fighting tears.

"We had a crash, Daddy," Brady replied dully.

Carter pulled back, but kept his arms around his children, unable to release them. "I know, buddy. I'm so sorry that happened."

"Where's Mommy?" Peyton asked in a thin voice.

Carter swallowed thickly. "The doctors are taking care of her right now. I'm sure we'll see her soon."

"She wouldn't wake up," Brady whispered, turning his face away, apparently to spare his sister. "I tried to wake her up, but she wouldn't wake up."

"It's okay. You did great," he replied. "I'm so glad you're both okay." He hugged his children tightly again.

"I called your parents," Stitch said quietly. "They should be here any minute. I can take the kids out to the waiting room so you can see Kenzie."

Carter nodded and thanked him, hugging his children once more before Stitch led them out. He stopped by the door to talk to a nurse, who nodded and quickly walked over to Carter.

"Mr. Reed? I can take you to your wife now."

Carter nodded again, too stunned to speak. They were supposed to be having pizza right now. They were supposed to be playing Candy Land. He was supposed to be making a pink gingerbread man for Peyton.

Instead he walked down a sterile hall smelling of disinfectant, unable to think or to speak.

All he could do was pray.

"Don't take her," he whispered over and over again under his breath. "Please, don't take her."

"She's in here," the nurse said quietly, pity and compassion in her eyes. "You don't have much time. They're prepping her for surgery."

Carter walked through the doorway to find a group of doctors and nurses surrounding his wife where she lay pale and small on a hospital bed. A smattering of cuts marred her skin along the right side of her face, and he could see similar abrasions on her right arm, above the splint.

"Kenzie?" Carter croaked, drawing the attention of everyone in the room. Everyone except Kenzie, whose eyes remained closed, her chest rising and falling slowly as she breathed.

"Mr. Reed? I'm Dr. Thomas." A tall African-American man in scrubs rounded the bed to approach him.

"How's Kenzie?" Carter asked.

The doctor frowned slightly. "She's got some broken bones—her leg, and a few ribs—but I'm afraid there are some internal injuries as well. We'll need to operate as soon as possible to deal with that."

"Operate?" Carter couldn't take his eyes from Kenzie's still frame.

"I'm sorry, I know this is a lot to take in," Dr. Thomas continued, "but we really don't have a lot of time. We need your consent for the surgery, sir." He held out a clipboard to Carter, who stared at it blankly before taking the offered pen and signing it.

"Can I talk to her?" he asked.

"She hasn't regained consciousness yet, but you can try," the doctor replied. "We'll give you a minute, then I'm afraid we'll have to take her to surgery." He motioned to the other staff and they all left the room, leaving Carter standing at the foot of the bed, gazing at his wife through unshed tears. Slowly, he approached her left side, taking her uninjured hand in his. He stroked the soft skin, kissing it gently and pressing it to his cheek.

"Kenzie?" he whispered. "Kenzie, don't leave me." He watched her intently. "Please don't leave me."

Kenzie's eyelids fluttered and her hand twitched in his. He watched in awe as her eyes opened slowly, staring unseeingly before she blinked and looked at him.

"Carter?"

Carter smiled, leaning forward to kiss her forehead softly. "Hey, baby."

She began to smile, wincing with pain. "I love it when you call me baby."

Carter chuckled. "I know."

"What happened?"

"There was an accident. God, Kenzie, I thought I lost you."

"Accident?" Kenzie's eyes grew alarmed. "The kids?"

"They're fine," he assured her. "They can't wait to see you."

Kenzie relaxed against the pillows, closing her eyes in relief. "Thank God."

Carter kissed her hand again. "I love you so much, Kenzie."

"I love you . . ." Kenzie's voice trailed off as a loud screeching sound burst from one of the machines.

"Kenzie?"

She didn't open her eyes. The doctors and nurses ran back into the room, shoving him out of the way unceremoniously.

"We can't wait," Dr. Thomas said urgently. "We've got to take her now!"

"What's happening? Kenzie?" Carter watched the frantic movements of the medical staff, panic and fear once again twisting in his stomach.

"One . . . two . . . three . . ." Dr. Thomas counted before they lifted Kenzie's body onto a gurney, laying her I.V. bag on her chest. They rolled her out into the hallway.

"I'm sorry, Mr. Reed, we have to go now," the doctor said as they rushed down the hallway. "I'll try to update you on her condition as soon as I can." They pushed Kenzie through a set of double doors and a nurse standing nearby grabbed his arm.

"Kenzie! I love you!" he called after her, his heart beating rapidly as his breathing seemed to stop. The thought of Kenzie going through those doors and never coming back—the thought of losing her forever—it gripped his chest like a vice. He turned to the nurse standing next to him, unaware that he had tears flowing down his cheeks.

"I'm sorry, you can't go in there," she said sympathetically. "You'll need to go to the waiting room." At his blank look, she turned him around, walking him through the door into the waiting area. He blinked unseeingly at his surroundings. Claire and David were playing with the children at a low table nearby. Noah, Lydia, Violet, and Macon spoke in low voices as they sipped bad coffee across the room.

Stitch sat by the door, stoic and silent, his back rigid, but his throat working constantly as he fought to maintain his control. They all looked up hopefully when he walked into the room.

"They took her to surgery," he said flatly, walking over to his children. He pulled them onto his lap and held them close, burying his nose in Peyton's hair.

"Daddy?" Brady looked up at him. "Is Mommy going to be okay?"

Carter stared down at his son for a moment, as the dazed fog over his brain finally lifted.

Wait.

Hold on. Just one minute.

What was he waiting for?

He set his children gently on the floor before standing up abruptly. "I'll be right back," he said, already searching his pockets as he headed for the hallway. He had to find an isolated spot.

You couldn't have angels popping up just anywhere.

He checked a few closed doors and finally found an empty patient's room. Pulling out the silver bell he rang it violently and waited.

"Hello, Carter."

He spun around to see Henry standing directly behind him.

"You have to save her," Carter said without preamble.

Henry gazed at him somberly. "I'm sorry. That's beyond my power."

"What do you mean?" Carter spat angrily. "You said the bell was for emergencies. This is a damned emergency! Save my wife."

"I can't, Carter."

"You won't."

"I *can't*," Henry repeated sadly. "Believe me, if I could do it, I would."

Deflated, Carter sat heavily on the bed. "Is she going to die?" he asked, his voice breaking.

Henry said nothing, but Carter could read the answer in his eyes.

"When?" he asked. "Today?"

Henry shook his head. "No, not today—not tomorrow—but soon. I can't give you an exact time. It's not up to me."

"So all this . . . it was all for nothing? I found Kenzie only to lose her again?"

"I'm sorry, Carter."

"You're sorry," he snarled sarcastically. "What kind of an angel are you, anyway?"

Henry smiled sadly. "I *can* do something else for you."

"What?"

"I can send you back."

"Back?" Carter repeated. "Back where? Back to New York?"

Henry nodded. "You can go back to that world. I can make you forget all this ever happened. No more pain . . . no sadness. You could have your old life back."

Carter stared at him disbelievingly. "What about my children?"

Henry shrugged lightly. "You won't remember them. I mean, you don't even believe they're real, do you?"

Did he?

He thought about teaching Brady to ride a bike, and learning how to hold Peyton's baby doll correctly. He thought about eating pancakes together and running on the beach.

He thought about hugs and kisses and baths and nighttime rituals.

Good night, sweet dreams

My love is in the moonbeams

And he thought about Kenzie . . . about living and loving and fighting and making up. He thought about sharing pizza and sharing laughs . . . about making love and building a life together.

Yes. It was *real*.

He believed it with all his heart.

"You have to decide now, Carter," Henry said. "I'm sorry, but it has to be now."

Carter didn't even think twice before he said simply, "No."

"No?"

"No." Carter stood up and squared his shoulders. "When Kenzie comes out of surgery, she's going to need me. If she is going to . . ." He cleared his throat and swallowed thickly. "If it's her time, I don't want her to be afraid. I want to be with her. The kids . . . the kids will need me to get through this. I have to be there for them."

Henry tilted his head, eyeing him carefully. "It's not going to be easy, Carter."

Carter nodded once. "I know that. But I can't give up on them. They need me and I'm not running away this time."

A bright smile broke out across Henry's face. "Excellent, Carter. Well done."

Suddenly the overhead lights began to glow brighter, until the whole room was filled with a dazzling light.

"What's happening?" Carter asked. Then, he knew.

"No!" he exclaimed.

"You've done really well, Carter . . . better than I expected, to be honest," Henry said proudly, the features of his face growing difficult to distinguish in the increasing light. Carter squinted, holding a hand up in front of him.

"No!" he said again. "You can't do this."

"Don't forget what you've learned, Carter," Henry admonished before the light exploded in Carter's eyes, blinding him momentarily.

He blinked hard a couple of times, trying to see the door leading out of the room. He had to get back to his family.

"Kenzie!" he cried out in a loud voice.

The next moment, he found himself sitting straight up in bed in his New York hotel room, fully dressed.

"No!" he exclaimed, looking around the room in disbelief. "Henry, you son of a— Damn it, send me back!" he screamed, searching his pockets for the bell. Not finding it, he tore the sheets off the bed, shaking them out before tossing them aside.

He dropped to the floor, running his hands frantically under the bed.

"Send me back, Henry!" he shouted.

The bell was gone. Henry was gone. His family was gone. Carter collapsed on the bare mattress, breathing heavily. After a moment, the sound of voices from the other room drew his attention. He walked out of the bedroom and into the little sitting area to find the television on, and *It's a Wonderful Life* playing yet again.

"Perfect," he mumbled, dropping to the floor against the front of the sofa, his head in his hands. "Kenzie," he moaned. "God, why?"

The people on the TV screen began to sing Auld Lang Syne as George Bailey held little Zuzu in his arms with a huge smile on his face. A bell rang on the Christmas tree and Zuzu pointed to it gleefully.

"Look, Daddy," the little girl said. *"Teacher says every time a bell rings, an angel gets his wings."*

"Yeah, well Teacher forgot to tell you that angels suck!" Carter shouted to the ceiling, hoping Henry was listening. He glanced back at the TV, fighting tears as the girl reminded him of his own daughter.

Mindless of the world around him, Carter curled up on the floor, mourning the life he'd lost.

Mourning the life he apparently never had.

Carter wallowed in misery for approximately twenty-three-point-four seconds.

Then, there was a loud and very insistent knock on the door.

chapter
SEVENTEEN
if you just believe

C arter tried to ignore whoever was at his door, but they would not be thwarted. The knocking continued, getting louder and louder until it became a rather obnoxious pounding.

"Go away," he grumbled under his breath where he lay on the floor. He repeated the command a little louder a moment later.

The knocking continued.

Finally, with an exasperated moan, Carter pulled himself to his feet, glaring at the credits of *It's a Wonderful Life* on the television as he made his way to the door. He whipped it open, staring in surprise at who he found standing there.

"Tess?"

"Morning, Carter," she said with a bright smile as she swept into the room. "Merry Christmas!"

"What?" He scrubbed his hands over his face, then up through his hair. "What are you doing here?"

"I came to drag you out of bed, of course," she said with a roll of her eyes. "You don't have much time. Goodness, did you sleep in those clothes?" She leaned toward him, her nose wrinkling. "Yeah. A shower's definitely in order, but you'll have to hurry."

"What are you talking about? How did you know where to find me? What are you doing here?" Carter repeated, his head still a little fuzzy.

Tess propped her fists on her hips, choosing to answer the second question first. "Your friend Henry told me where you were staying. I ran into him at the party last night."

"Party?"

"At the *Four Seasons* . . ." she prodded, "Mackenzie Monroe . . . You running out like a scared little girl . . . Ringing any bells?"

At the mention of bells, Carter's eyes narrowed. "You said Henry sent you here?"

"Yeah," she said grabbing his arm and steering him toward the bedroom. "I met him at the party and he mentioned he knew you. When I found out about that guy you saw with Kenzie, I knew I had to come find you."

"Guy? What guy? What are you talking about?" Carter planted his feet on the plush carpet. "What's going on?"

"He's gay, Carter."

"Gay? Who? Henry?" Carter's head was spinning.

"No, not Henry." She laughed. "Martin."

Carter rubbed his temples, trying to ward off the headache he could feel coming on. "Who the hell's Martin?"

Tess waved her hands in exasperation. "The guy you saw with Kenzie last night. Aren't you listening?"

"I'm listening. It's just a little hard to keep up."

"Yeah. I get that a lot," she said with a slight frown. "Anyway, I got to meet her last night. She really is amazing, and so nice! She told me to call her Kenzie, isn't that sweet? She autographed my book—well, your book." Tess pulled the novel out of her shoulder bag and handed it to Carter. He reached out slowly to take it. "I told her all about you."

"You did what?"

"She was *really* interested, Carter," Tess continued in a rather enticing voice. "She kept asking questions about you."

"Okay, enough," Carter said gruffly. "Tell me what this is all about. Now," he ordered. At Tess's wide-eyed look, he sighed. "Please."

Tess huffed slightly. "It's simple, Carter. Kenzie is not involved with that guy Martin. He's just a friend she takes to events so she doesn't have to be alone. She's lonely, Carter. She misses you."

"She said that?"

"Oh for heaven's sake. Men are such idiots!" Tess exclaimed, slugging him in the shoulder lightly. "Of course she didn't *say* it, but it was very obvious. I could see it on her face whenever I said your name."

Carter collapsed onto the sofa, reaching up to clutch at his hair. "What do I do?" he asked finally, his head still spinning.

She'd met Henry, which meant he was real.

Which meant his other life was real. Didn't it?

Or maybe . . . maybe it was a lesson . . . a warning.

"She's staying at the *Four Seasons*, but she told me she's catching a flight later this morning," Tess told him. "She's heading home to visit her family for Christmas. Now's your chance to catch her before she leaves."

Kenzie was here . . . in the here and now.

Maybe it wasn't too late.

At Carter's dazed look, Tess narrowed her eyes. "It's been ten years. Have you learned *nothing*, Carter?" she asked quietly.

Carter stiffened at that. All was not lost. In this life, there was still a chance . . . but he had to take it. He couldn't let it slip away.

"There's not much time," she added. "What's it gonna be, Carter?"

I'm not running away this time.

Carter shot to his feet. "Do I have time for a shower?"

Tess smiled brightly. "Yes, but make it fast. No time to shave. The scruffy look's kind of sexy anyway." She shoved him into the bathroom and closed the door behind him. "And do that tousled thing you do with your hair," she called through the door. "Women love that."

"I don't know what you're talking about," he called back as he stepped under the spray.

Carter thought he might have heard her mutter something derogatory about men on the other side of the door, but he couldn't be sure. He showered quickly, scrubbing his hair with a towel after wiping the steam from the mirror. He frowned at the damp mop, running his hand through it quickly.

Tousled? He twisted a few sandy strands, but they bounced back to their customary position—wild and uncontrollable.

"Carter, hurry up!" Tess yelled impatiently. Carter shrugged at his reflection and walked into the bedroom, a towel draped around his hips.

Tess had apparently gone through his luggage while he was in the shower. A set of clothes lay on the bed—underwear, socks, jeans, and a white cotton shirt.

"Making yourself at home, I see," he shouted into the other room as he pulled on the shirt.

"Just get dressed, Carter. We don't have time for this," she hollered back.

Carter threw on his clothes, slid his feet into his favorite pair of worn boots, and grabbed a wool coat from the closet.

"You're much pushier than I remember from last night," he said as he shrugged into the coat and picked up his old leather satchel, tucking Kenzie's book inside.

Tess shrugged. "Just part of my charm. Now come on, let's go already," she ordered.

They hurried to the elevator and Tess pressed the button for the underground garage. "I brought my car," she explained. "Didn't want to have to wait for a cab." She checked her watch. "We should make it just in time."

When the elevator doors opened, they ran through the parking garage, Carter trailing after Tess as she dodged between the parked cars. He stifled a laugh when she came to a stop next to a huge purple Lincoln.

"Hey," she said defensively, "don't mock the Lincoln. It's a classic."

"I didn't say a word," Carter replied, holding his hands up in front of him. "Can you even drive this thing in New York?"

Tess patted the roof affectionately as she unlocked the door.

"When people see this baby coming, they get out of the way," she said.

"I'll bet."

Tess handled the monstrous car with ease, pulling effortlessly out of the garage and into traffic. Carter was surprised to see that she was right. People did get out of the way.

"Why are you doing this?" he asked quietly as she sped past a cab, pulling in front of it quickly and ignoring the horn blaring behind her.

"He was going too slow," she replied absently.

"No," Carter clarified with a laugh. "I mean, why are you helping me? We hardly know each other."

"Oh, that." Tess smiled widely. "Guess I'm just a sucker for love."

She skidded around a corner and screeched to a stop in front of the *Four Seasons*.

"Okay, you're up," she said brightly as Carter's stomach turned somersaults. "Go get your girl, Carter."

He reached for the door handle and stepped out onto the sidewalk, ducking his head back inside before closing it.

"No matter what happens, thank you, Tess," he said.

She waved a hand. "Just don't let her get away again, okay?"

Carter nodded and shut the door, turning to jog toward the hotel's entrance. He heard Tess gun the Lincoln's engine, and then she was gone.

He was on his own. Where should he start? His mind raced as he wove through a crowd of people walking out the entry doors. Would the desk clerk even tell him which room Kenzie was in? Carter would have to be persistent. Hell, he'd wait in the lobby until she showed up if he had to.

He'd find a way.

Squaring his shoulders, Carter pulled open the glass door, holding it for a group of people coming out, politeness winning out over impatience.

Then he saw her.

She passed within inches of him, pulling a rolling suitcase, her attention on a telephone call.

"No, I'm leaving the hotel now," she said as the scent of her perfume wafted toward his nose. It was different than he remembered, but somehow uniquely Kenzie.

Had it only been a few hours since they lay in bed together, whispering in the darkness? Fewer still since he held her hand and told her he loved her?

Carter could barely take a breath. His heart clenched in his chest, as though unwilling to pump blood through his body. He could hardly believe she was there in front of him—alive and well—almost close enough to touch if he reached out.

"Yes, I'll have to deal with it when I get to Woodlawn," she said as she approached a black town car waiting at the curb, unaware of Carter trailing behind her. "Yes . . . yes, I'll call you when I land . . . okay . . . okay! Sheesh, cut me a break, Maddie, it's Christmas!" Kenzie handed her suitcase to the driver and turned back toward the hotel.

"Yes, yes, I promise I'll—" Her words cut off abruptly, her eyes widening as she finally noticed Carter standing just a few feet away.

He took a step toward her. "Kenzie."

Her mouth opened and closed a few times, no sound coming forth. Finally, she blinked, shaking her head slightly. Carter could hear whoever was on the other end of the phone talking rapidly.

"Mad, I'll have to call you back," Kenzie said quietly, hanging up without waiting for an answer.

They stood for a moment, staring at each other. Kenzie finally cleared her throat. "Carter. It's . . . it's been a long time."

Carter licked his lips, taking another step toward her. "Too long."

"How have you been?" she asked, feigning nonchalance, but Carter recognized the telltale flush on her cheeks, the bite of her lip that proved her nervousness.

"Honestly? Not good, Kenzie. Not good for a very long time," he admitted.

"I'm sorry to hear that," she said, her voice cracking slightly. She cleared her throat and looked away for a moment. "Carter, what are you doing here?"

"I came to find you."

"Me? Why?" Her chin lifted slightly, and Carter recognized the flash of anger in her eyes. "It's been ten years, Carter. Why come find me now?"

Carter took a deep breath.

All in.

Now or never.

"I miss you," he told her, taking another step closer. "I love you."

She stared at him in shock, and he took advantage of her speechlessness. "I know it took me a while to figure it out," he continued quickly, now close enough to touch her. He didn't, though. He didn't want to scare her off. Instead, his eyes raked over her face, taking in the familiar curve of her cheek . . . the stain of pink on her chilled skin . . . the flutter of her hair in the icy breeze.

"I'm sorry it took so long," he continued, "but if you'll give me a chance, I swear I'll make it up to you, Kenzie."

She looked away, the wind blowing her hair back from her face. Carter stared at her, unable to take his eyes off her. He half feared that if he did, she would disappear.

"What makes you think I feel the same?" she asked, crossing her arms over her chest. "It's been a long time. Things are different now."

"I know," he said. "I know I have no right to ask you for anything. But I am. I'm asking."

She blinked at him, her eyes soft, scared. "You really hurt me," she said.

"I know," he replied softly. "I know I did, and I'm so sorry. It's the biggest regret of my life. But someone told me recently that second chances aren't about fixing mistakes as much as learning from them.

"I've learned, Kenzie. I've learned what it means to really love someone." She turned back to him and he prayed he was getting through. "I've learned that it's not all about romantic gestures and fancy words," he said fervently. "It's about doing the laundry and paying the bills. It's about raising a family and being there to tuck your kids into bed at night. It's about day in and day out living life together . . . through the good times and the bad.

"For a long time I regretted what happened between us. But I was so paralyzed by what happened *then* that I couldn't see the possibilities of *now*. I was so wrapped up in thinking about what might have been that I couldn't see what *could be*."

"Carter, it's been ten years," Kenzie said again, crossing her arms over her chest. "Sure, I was hurt at the time . . . for a long time, actually, but I got over it. I've moved on."

"Have you?" he asked, leaning toward her, his eyes searching hers for the truth. "Because if you really have, I'll go. If you can tell me that it's really over—that you don't have any feelings left for me—that there's no chance for us anymore, I'll go, Kenzie, and I won't bother you again.

"But if there is a *chance*," he said softly. "If there's a possibility that we could build something together here . . . *now* . . . please don't turn away from it. I'll fight for us, Kenzie. I'll do whatever it takes if you'll give me a chance—give *us* a chance.

"We could have an amazing life, Kenzie. I've *seen* it. I've seen what we can be together when we really try to make it work, and it's amazing. You wouldn't believe it . . . how amazing it is." He reached out, taking her chilled hand in both of his. "Just a beginning. That's all I'm asking for. We could go have breakfast—or a cup of coffee— whatever you want."

Kenzie opened her mouth to reply, but was interrupted by her driver who was standing on the other side of the Town Car. "Excuse me, Miss Monroe," he said quietly, earning a glare from Carter, which he ignored. "I'm sorry to interrupt, but we need to leave now if we're going to get to the airport on time."

Kenzie nodded, turning back to Carter. "I'm sorry, I have to go," she said quietly. "I'm going home for Christmas."

Carter held her hand a little tighter. "Okay . . . yes, I understand," he said, adding hopefully, "When will you be back? Can I see you then?"

"No." She shook her head and Carter's heart fell. "No, I mean, I won't be back in New York . . . not anytime soon," she clarified. "I'll be in

Woodlawn until New Year's, then I start a book tour."

"Oh." Carter couldn't hide his disappointment.

"Unless," she began hesitantly. "I mean . . . I suppose, if you wanted to . . . you could . . . come?"

A new hope bloomed in Carter's chest. "To Woodlawn?"

"Yeah." Kenzie shrugged. "I know you're probably too busy—"

"No . . . no, I'm not too busy," Carter said quickly. "I don't go back to work until the New Year."

"But you don't have any luggage. I suppose you could take a later flight," she suggested.

"No," Carter said firmly. At her surprised look, he smiled softly. "Now that I've found you, I'm not letting you out of my sight. I can get clothes in Woodlawn. I know they have great flannel there."

Kenzie laughed. "Flannel? Doesn't really sound like your style."

"You'd be surprised," he said with a grin.

Kenzie looked up at him as the driver opened the car door. "What's happened to you, Carter?"

"It's a long story," he told her with a deep breath.

"Sir?" The driver held his hand out to Carter. "I think you dropped this."

Carter extended his palm and the man dropped a little metal ball into it. Carter stared at it for a moment in shock.

A silver bell.

"Where did you get this?" he asked.

The driver shrugged. "It fell out of your pocket."

Carter took the bell between his fingers, shaking it gently. It tinkled lightly and Carter held his breath, his eyes scanning the area.

Nothing.

"Carter? Are you coming?" Kenzie asked from inside the car. Carter looked down at her, a smile growing as he realized the gift he'd been given. A do over. A new beginning. He tucked the bell into his jeans pocket and slid into the seat next to her.

As they pulled away from the curb, Kenzie turned toward him. "So, this long story . . ." she prodded.

Carter grinned. "Oh, it's pretty unbelievable," he said. "It's got angels and miracles. As a matter of fact," he said speculatively, "it could make a good book."

Kenzie settled into the seat. "Well, that sounds like a story I'd like to hear."

So he told her.

As they drove to the airport and waited in the VIP lounge, Kenzie listened raptly as Carter told the story . . . stopping only when they had to check her bag or show their tickets or when it was time to board. Carter managed to switch seats with an older man so he could sit next to Kenzie and once the plane took off, she asked him impatiently, "And then what happened?"

He told his story without holding back any of the crazy-sounding details. Kenzie interrupted occasionally only to ask questions.

"How old was Peyton?"

"Lydia and Noah were *married*?"

"Really? Violet and Macon Bridges?"

Carter answered her questions patiently, and somewhere over the Midwest, he finished his rather remarkable tale, taking Kenzie up to the moment that he woke up in his hotel room.

"You're right," she said with a sigh, sitting back in her seat. "That is quite a story." She looked at him thoughtfully. "So, it was all a dream then?"

Carter shook his head slowly. "No. No, I don't think so. I don't know how, but it was real. At least to me."

"So . . . what happened to all of them?" she asked. "Are they still out there somewhere?"

Carter shrugged. "I don't know for sure," he replied. "I think maybe they were all part of . . . a *possibility*. What would have been—*could* have been—if things had gone differently between us back then."

"That's kind of sad," she mused. "It's like they had to be sacrificed for us to have this chance."

"Isn't every choice like that?" Carter asked.

"I suppose."

"You seem to be taking this awfully well," he said wryly. "Don't you think I'm crazy?"

Kenzie laughed. "Crazy? Definitely."

Carter smirked. "Well, you're the one that invited the crazy person home," he pointed out.

"True," she admitted, "but in my defense, that was before you told me what happened."

Carter sobered. "So what do you think . . . really?"

Kenzie smiled at him softly. "I think something definitely happened to you last night," she said. "Whether it was a dream or a magical trip to an alternate reality . . . who can know for sure? *There are more things in Heaven and Earth . . .*"

" *. . . than are dreamt of in your Philosophy,*" Carter concluded the quote from Hamlet.

"Yeah." Kenzie grinned. "There are so many mysteries out there, Carter. It's part of what makes life exciting, isn't it?"

Carter smiled, taking her hand and lifting it to his lips. "Thanks."

"For what?"

"For not calling me crazy."

"I'm just glad you're here," Kenzie said softly.

"Me, too."

They sat in silence for a while, both gazing out the window at the clouds floating by, lost in their own thoughts.

"It *had* to be real," Carter said after a moment. At Kenzie's questioning look, he continued, "Tess said she met Henry . . . so he couldn't have been a figment of my imagination, right?"

"Who's Tess?"

"You met her at the party last night," Carter told her. "You talked to her about me."

Kenzie's brow creased in confusion. "I didn't talk to anyone about you last night."

"Sure you did." Carter thought maybe Kenzie had forgotten amidst all the people she'd met at the party. "Tall girl? Pink hair? Kinda looks like a unicorn?"

At Kenzie's shrug, Carter reached under his seat for his satchel. "She's a big fan of yours. You signed a book for her," he said, pulling it out and flipping it open. He turned a few pages, looking for the autograph. "I don't understand," he murmured as he searched the book, slamming it shut as the search came up empty. "She said she talked to you. She convinced me that I should come find you. She knew all about that guy Martin, and said that you missed me."

"I did miss you," Kenzie said with a small smile.

Carter squeezed her hand. "But how did she know that if she never talked to you?"

They stared at each other for a moment.

"You don't think . . ." Kenzie began. "Maybe Henry wasn't working alone?"

"Maybe." Carter replied. "Or maybe I just imagined them both."

"You don't really believe that."

Carter shrugged. "I don't know. I don't know anything except whatever happened—whatever it was that led me to this moment—I owe to the two of them."

Kenzie smiled at him. "I guess I owe them, too."

Carter lifted his arm around her shoulders, drawing her close to his side. "I know we can't just pick up where we left off, Kenzie," he said quietly. "We have a lot to catch up on . . . a lot to learn about each other."

"We have plenty of time," she replied. She picked up his other hand and played idly with his fingers.

"I wonder how it ends," Kenzie murmured after a while.

"What?"

"The story," she said, turning toward him again with a smile, her eyes twinkling. "It *would* make a great book, but it needs an ending."

"Well, I'd say that's up to you," Carter replied.

Kenzie tapped her lips thoughtfully. "It can't end with them up in the air," she mused. "I mean, it's so unresolved."

Carter smirked. "Good point." He leaned closer to her, his eyes dipping to her lips. "Maybe he'll lean in, promise to love her forever, and kiss her passionately."

Kenzie fought a grin, wrinkling her nose. "That's kind of cliché, don't you think?" She blushed, though. The blush always gave her away.

He reached out with one hand to cup her face, savoring the feel of her warm skin as he brushed his thumb along her cheekbone. "Clichés become clichés for a reason," he pointed out, his lips a mere breath away from hers. "I prefer to think of it as a classic . . . a crowd pleaser."

"You think?" Kenzie asked breathlessly. She licked her lips, leaning slightly into his hand.

"Oh, yeah . . . definitely," Carter murmured, almost able to taste her already. "Everyone loves a happy ending."

Then he kissed her.

And Kenzie didn't think it was cliché at all.

EPILOGUE

joy to the world

Christmas Eve, Two Years Later

"I hope they're okay," Kenzie murmured to Carter as she looked out the window of their New York apartment onto the snow-covered streets below. "Maybe we should have gone to the airport to get them."

Carter wrapped his arms around Kenzie's waist—a difficult task given the late stages of her pregnancy. He rubbed her swollen belly, smiling at the feel of a kick under his palm.

"I offered, but we couldn't fit them all in the car anyway," Carter replied. "They'll be fine. Don't worry so much."

But Kenzie was worried. Given her condition, she and Carter couldn't fly back to Woodlawn for the holidays and she'd been disappointed that they wouldn't get to see their families. Carter, however, had taken the opportunity to use some of his abundant frequent flier miles to buy tickets for them all to come to New York instead. Kenzie had

211

cried when he told her. Of course, Kenzie was especially prone to crying lately, but that didn't diminish the fact that she was overwhelmed and so thankful for what Carter had done.

A winter storm had caused some problems, however. The connecting flight was delayed, and the tired group was forced to stay overnight in Chicago. Once the runways were cleared, they were back in the air, but Kenzie knew she wouldn't feel completely at ease until they were all safe and warm together.

She searched the streets again and Carter kissed the top of her head. "Relax. I just checked, and the plane landed safely. The rental car has four-wheel drive. They'll be fine."

The phone rang and Carter squeezed Kenzie once more before releasing her and crossing the room to answer it. Kenzie watched him anxiously as he spoke, and Carter smiled and nodded at her in reassurance.

"They're on the way," he said once he'd hung up the phone. "They dropped their luggage at the hotel and should be here in a few minutes."

Kenzie nodded in acknowledgement. "Did you put the fresh towels in the guest room?" she asked nervously.

"Yes. It's all ready," Carter replied indulgently. Although they would have enjoyed having the whole family stay with them at the apartment, there just wasn't enough room. Fortunately, there was a nice hotel only a few blocks away, so at least everyone would be close.

Kenzie stretched, pressing her hands to her lower back with a slight groan.

"Tired?" Carter asked, moving behind her to massage her aching muscles.

"A little," she admitted, "My back is killing me today."

"Hmmm . . ." Carter murmured, rubbing circles into her back with his thumbs. "Maybe after we get everyone settled you can have a nice bath."

She leaned back into him. "That sounds wonderful." The sound of a buzzer interrupted their quiet moment, and Kenzie straightened quickly. "They're here!" she exclaimed, hurrying over to answer the buzz.

"Hello?"

"Merry Christmas!" A chorus of voices crackled over the loudspeaker. Stitch's voice then added, "Let us in. It's freezing out here!"

Kenzie laughed and buzzed them in, opening the door so she could watch for them coming down the hallway. Carter stood next to her, his arm over her shoulders.

"Excited?" he asked. She looked up with glowing eyes and popped up on her tiptoes to offer him a smacking kiss.

"This is the best Christmas gift ever!" she told him, turning back down the hallway as the elevator doors opened.

Then they were there . . . and the sounds of laughter and "I missed you" and "Merry Christmases" filled the hallway as they all made their way into the apartment.

"Hope you're all hungry," Kenzie announced once they'd all settled inside.

"Starved," David and Stitch said simultaneously, causing another round of laughter.

Carter and Kenzie had set up a buffet of finger foods and Christmas treats, and the group filled their plates and took their seats in the living room in front of the crackling fire, and a brightly lit Christmas tree.

Carter found it difficult to eat. Instead, he looked around the room, considering how his life had changed in the past two years.

First, there was Kenzie. His eyes lingered on his wife, glowing and radiant in the light from the Christmas tree. It reminded him of when he first saw her in New York at the party at the *Four Seasons* . . . before his life had taken it's rather unusual turn.

But she looked different now, too. Of course, she was still beautiful, but as Carter caught her eye and a genuine smile lit her face, his breath caught—as it often did when he saw her smile.

She was his. And she was happy. It was everything he wanted. His eyes trailed down to her belly. Well, almost everything.

Theirs had been a whirlwind courtship. After the week they spent together in Woodlawn, they both knew they didn't want to waste any more time. He'd had to return to New York for his new job, and Kenzie went on her book tour, but they spoke every night—either on the phone or on the Internet. Carter smiled at the thoughts of some of their more interesting Web dates.

God bless Skype.

She'd come back to New York for Valentine's Day and Carter knew he couldn't wait any longer. He proposed on one knee in front of the *Four Seasons*, offering her his heart and a diamond ring. She'd cried and smiled and said yes. They were married six months later, to the delight of their families. Well, to the delight of Carter's family anyway. Sheriff Monroe was his usual restrained self, although Carter felt he was warming to him.

Stitch caught Carter's considering look and his eyes narrowed.

Okay. Maybe not.

They loved their little apartment, but with the baby coming they decided they'd need something bigger. In the spring, they would close escrow on their new house. Yes, Carter was leaving Manhattan and moving to the suburbs.

He even had a few flannel shirts.

He and Kenzie would miss the city, but they both agreed it would be better for the children. Well, *child* for now, but Carter was hopeful. They both were.

Kenzie could write anywhere, of course, and had decided to cut back on traveling and book tours once the baby arrived. That was one good thing about her success—she no longer *had* to promote herself. Her books kind of sold themselves.

Especially her most recent one. *The Do Over* had debuted at number one on the *New York Times* Bestsellers list and stayed there for twelve weeks.

Carter was right . . . people did love a happy ending.

As for his job at the network, Carter was enjoying staying closer to home. Once they moved, he would have to commute into the city, and he'd still have to travel occasionally, but he knew they would make it work.

It was something he'd come to grasp only recently—the fact that he and Kenzie were better able to deal with the challenges of their life together now than they were all those years ago. They'd both had the opportunities to grow—both professionally and personally—over the decade they were apart.

If anything, it made them appreciate each other more, now that they'd found each other again.

Carter's eyes moved to his sister where she sat next to Noah Collins. The sight of them together made him smile. Carter and Kenzie had made sure the two were seated next to each other at their wedding reception. It had taken very little encouragement for them to realize they were meant for each other.

They planned to get married the following summer.

As for Violet, it had taken a little more convincing to get her to give Macon Bridges a chance. You sure couldn't tell it now, though. Carter smiled at the dreamy way she was looking up at Macon as he dramatically told a story about the hotel where they stayed in Chicago. He and Vi had been living together for about four months, and seemed to be incredibly happy.

Carter's gaze landed on his parents, and he searched for the right word to describe how they felt about becoming grandparents. *Thrilled* was too tame. *Ecstatic* was closer, but still didn't quite suffice. He and Kenzie had decided to start a family as soon as possible, and his parents were the first people they told when they found out she was pregnant. He knew they'd be frequent visitors once the baby arrived, even if they did live on the other side of the country.

Out of the corner of his eye, he saw Kenzie wince. He slid closer to her on the sofa, reaching out to rub her back. "You okay, baby?" he asked, leaning close to murmur in her ear.

Kenzie nodded. "Yeah. Just tired. Too much excitement I guess," she replied with a weak smile.

"Let's get you that bath and to bed," he said quietly. "The family will understand."

Kenzie nodded again, laying her plate on the coffee table as Carter helped her up.

"Everything okay?" David asked in concern.

Carter smiled, continuing to rub Kenzie's sore back. "Yeah. The baby's just telling Kenzie she needs some rest."

"Carter?" Kenzie's trembling voice drew his attention.

"Yeah, baby?"

"I don't think I need rest," she said hesitantly.

"But you said you were tired."

"Uh . . . yeah . . ."

"Kenzie, what's wrong?"

"Umm . . . I think it's time."

"Time for what?"

"*Time* time."

Carter stared at her blankly for a moment. "What?" he said finally, his heart beginning to pound in his chest. "Are you sure? Isn't it too soon?"

"Uh," Kenzie said nervously, gripping his arm as her face clenched in pain. "Considering the fact that I think my water just broke, yeah, I'm pretty sure."

"It's time!" Carter exclaimed. "Holy crap, it's time!"

"You already said that," Kenzie said with a wry smile that quickly turned to a grimace.

In that instant, the room erupted in chaos.

"What do we do?"

"Kenzie, maybe you should sit down."

"We need to get to the hospital."

"Boil some water!"

"Okay, everyone hold it!" Stitch's voice took on that "sheriff" tone of authority and the room was suddenly silent. He turned to Carter. "Does Kenzie have a bag packed?"

Carter nodded dumbly.

"Okay, go get it." He turned to David. "You. Get Carter's car. Macon, get the rental. Lydia, help Kenzie get some dry clothes, but make it fast."

Lydia took Kenzie's arm gingerly and led her into the bedroom. Kenzie called out over her shoulder. "The doctor's number is by the phone, would someone please call him?"

Vi was assigned that task, and within a few minutes, David pulled up in Carter's car and Carter, Kenzie, and Claire piled in. They took off toward the hospital, the rest of the group following behind in the rental car.

"Oh God, Carter, it hurts!" Kenzie moaned from the back seat, where he held her hand, stroking her hair back from her face.

"I know, baby," he replied, working hard to keep the panic out of his voice as David sped down the icy streets. "Do the breathing . . . like in class, remember?" He breathed along with Kenzie as he prayed he'd get them all to the hospital safely.

They pulled up in front of the emergency entrance and Carter had a brief, agonizing flashback to the last time he'd been to an ER. One look at Kenzie's pained face pushed that memory away, though.

She needed him. He wasn't going to let her down. He took her hand as a nurse helped Kenzie into a wheelchair. "It's going to be okay, baby," he murmured, pressing a kiss to her forehead and taking her hand. "You can do this. I'll be with you the whole time."

Kenzie nodded, breathing deeply as Carter turned to the nurse. "We're already pre-registered," he told her. "Dr. Jenkins is on the way."

The next few minutes were a blur of nurses and machines and breathing and moans. When the doctor swept in, and after a brief examination, announced it was time to head to the delivery room, Carter's heart stopped, then sped along crazily.

"It's time, Kenzie," Carter whispered, as they rolled her down the hallway. "He'll be here soon."

"Carter, I'm scared."

"I know, baby. I'm scared, too," he confessed. "Hold my hand. You can do it. It's almost over."

Carter looked into Kenzie's eyes as the doctor said, "Now, Kenzie. Push now!"

He held her hand as she gritted her teeth, bearing down again and again as she fought to bring a new life into the world.

"Stop now, Kenzie. Don't push for a minute," the doctor said. Kenzie turned crazed eyes to Carter.

"Almost there, baby," he encouraged, kissing her hand. "I love you so much."

"I love you, too," she said weakly. "But if you ever do this to me again, I'm going to kill you."

Carter couldn't keep back a snort of laughter.

The doctor's firm voice cut into their bubble. "Okay, Kenzie. One more should do it, on the next contraction, push hard. Let's say hello to this little guy, okay?"

Carter held her hand, but as she pushed, he couldn't keep his eyes on hers. Instead, they drifted down to the doctor . . . to his hands between his wife's legs . . . to the miracle he was witnessing before his very eyes.

One second the doctor's hands were empty. The next, they were filled with a wiggling mass of arms and legs.

"Oh my God," Carter breathed. "He's here."

"It's a boy," Dr. Jenkins announced.

"Is he okay?" Kenzie asked, struggling up onto her elbows so she could see her son.

"He's perfect," the doctor assured her.

A nurse wiped the little boy off a little before wrapping him up and handing him to his mother.

"Oh!" Kenzie exclaimed. "He's so pretty!"

Carter chuckled. "Boy's aren't pretty, Kenzie," he corrected, blinking through tears as he looked down at the sleeping child.

"Well, he is," Kenzie said stubbornly, her own tears trickling down her cheeks. "He's beautiful."

Carter leaned down to kiss her. "Yeah, he is," he admitted.

They both stared at their new son, not even noticing the staff working in the room, or when they finally left to give them some privacy.

"Thank you," Carter told Kenzie quietly. "I can't—"

Carter never finished his sentence, because at that moment, his son opened his eyes. Like all babies', they were kind of gray, but in that instant, Carter knew they would be brown.

Dark brown, like his mother's.

"What is it?" Kenzie asked.

"It's . . . it's *him*." Carter's voice was full of awe. His son looked up at him and Carter couldn't explain it, but he *knew* him. He *recognized* him.

"Him?" Kenzie repeated. "You don't mean . . . it can't be . . ."

Carter turned to her, his eyes once again filling with tears. "It is. I don't know how it's possible, but it is."

Kenzie looked down at her son, turning him in her arms so she could look into his face.

"Hello, Brady," she said, her own voice cracking with emotion. "It's nice to finally meet you. I've heard so much about you, sweetie."

"Brady," Carter breathed, his heart nearly bursting with the realization that the son he thought he'd left behind . . . that he had begun to doubt ever really existed at all, was right in front of him. "I missed you, buddy." He touched the little boy's hand, and Brady wrapped a chubby fist around Carter's finger. Carter grinned through his tears, suddenly sure that in a couple of years he'd be back in a room like this, meeting a little girl with crazy blond hair and hazel eyes like his.

"Mrs. Reed?" A nurse walked into the room tentatively. "Your family's asking to see the baby. Is it all right if I show them in?"

Kenzie smiled brightly. "Yes, of course. He needs to meet his family."

They came in with bright smiles and tears, passing little Brady around from aunt to uncle to grandpa to a very possessive grandma. They welcomed him to the world with gift shop flowers and balloons and a huge teddy bear. And before they left in the early morning hours to try and get some much deserved sleep, they each said goodbye with a gentle touch to his little head or a kiss to his cheek.

The boy would be loved.

When the room was quiet again, Kenzie drifted off, and Carter picked up his son and carried him to the windows overlooking the city.

"We're going to have so much fun," Carter promised him. "I swear you can count on me. I won't let you down."

Another thing Carter was grateful for—among the many things Carter was grateful for—was that he still had his grandfather's cufflinks in this life. He hadn't given the heirlooms much thought when he'd impulsively jumped on that plane two years earlier. Not that he wouldn't do the same thing again, but he was happy he remembered about them once they landed. A quick call to the hotel had secured his possessions until he returned to New York—including the little box he kept tucked deep in his duffle bag. One day, he'd pass the cufflinks on to Brady, along with the pocket watch . . . and a certain little silver bell.

Brady fussed, his mouth rooting around, and Carter turned to wake Kenzie.

She opened sleepy eyes, holding her arms out to take the baby and settling him against her breast.

Carter stood with his hands in his pockets, looking down on his wife as she nursed his infant son. He fingered the little bell he now kept on his key ring, a constant reminder that sometimes life took funny turns . . . that love was always worth fighting for . . .

And that miracles happened every day.

Outside Room 665 at Lenox Hill Hospital, a blond man and a pink-haired woman stood together in the hallway, watching the events inside the little hospital room with smiles on their faces. People passing by avoided bumping into them, kept away by an unseen force, although they didn't really *see* them.

They *could* have seen them, if they were looking. But people so rarely *really* looked.

"Brady?" Tess questioned, turning to the man standing next to her. "Did you do that?"

Henry shrugged. "That's above my paygrade," he said simply.

Tess smiled, her attention drawn back by a laugh inside the room. Carter had settled on the side of the bed, playing with his son's fingers, and smiling at Kenzie.

"I'm glad we came back," she murmured quietly. "It's nice to see things are working out for them."

"Yeah," Henry replied. "There's something special about them, isn't there?" He watched for a moment before tilting his head toward the exit. "Come on. It's time to go."

Tess turned to walk down the hallway, taking one last look at the happy family before she stepped away.

"You did a good job," Henry stated as they made their way to the stairs.

Tess's gaze snapped to him. "Thanks," she said with a bright smile, reaching out to loop her arm through his. "Does that mean I'll get my own assignment soon?"

Henry rolled his eyes. "You tired of working with me already?"

"No, it's not that," she said playfully, hugging his arm as they walked out onto the streets of New York. "It's just . . . after all the training I've had, it would be nice to know that someone has some confidence in my abilities. Get a chance to spread my wings, so to speak."

Henry laughed, taking a deep breath of the crisp winter air. "Like I haven't heard that before," he said. "You know it's not up to me. I'm sure you'll get your chance when it's time. Just be patient."

"Like I haven't heard *that* before," Tess muttered.

"Look," Henry said softly, distracting Tess from her thoughts. She looked to the horizon, where the first light of dawn was peeking over the skyline. "No matter how many times I see it, it always takes my breath away," he added.

They stood quietly amidst the bustling city streets, ignoring the crowds and the cars. Their eyes were on the sky, watching the twisting and twirling ribbons of color—pinks and oranges and yellows finally giving way to pale blue as the new day broke.

Their minds were on the little family back at the hospital that was just starting a new life together.

Henry took a deep breath. "Perfect," he said, leaning down to press a kiss to the top of Tess's head. "Merry Christmas, Tess."

She smiled sunnily back up at him.

"Merry Christmas, Daddy."

also by
T.M. FRANKLIN

The MORE Trilogy
"Reminiscent of the Mortal Instruments Series...
only better!" - Penny Dreadful Reviews
MORE | The Guardians | TWELVE

The *How to Survive High School* Series
"Looking for a sweet first love tale? This is your
book. You won't be sorry."
- Laurie A., Amazon Reviewer
How to Get Ainsley Bishop To Fall in Love with
You
***Coming Soon* – How to Get Viney Palmari a**
Date for the Prom

Cutlass
"It's a rollercoaster ride from start to finish - with
treasure maps, sword fights, and of course an
enemies-to-lovers romance that made me swoon.
Beautifully written, it kept me hooked right until
the end." - Carrie, Amazon Reviewer

A Piece of Cake
Unscheduled Departure
Short and sweet romances with a mystical touch.

ACKNOWLEDGMENTS

Many thanks to my wonderful editor, Kathie Spitz and my proofreader, Rose David. I couldn't do any of this without you!

Thanks also to the T.M. Franklin Book Club for helping to spread the word about my books, and to the many bloggers and readers who do the same.
Thanks to the awesome authors of Enchanted Publications - Jeanne McDonald, Sydney Logan, Lindsey Gray, Jennifer Locklear, Melanie Moreland, Carrie Elks, Jo Richardson, Jiffy Kate, Jami Denise, Ayden K. Morgen, Alexix Riddley and Cara Dee. Be sure and check out their books!

And thanks most of all to my family for their unceasing love and support.

about the
AUTHOR

T.M. Franklin writes stories of adventure, romance, & a little magic. A former TV news producer, she decided making stuff up was more fun than reporting the facts. Her first published novel, MORE, was born during National Novel Writing month, a challenge to write a novel in thirty days. MORE was well-received, being selected as a finalist in the 2013 Kindle Book Review Best Indie Book Awards, as well as winning the Suspense/Thriller division of the Blogger Book Fair Reader's Choice Awards. She's since written three additional novels and several best-selling short stories...and there's always more on the way.

Connect with T.M. Franklin at her website:
www.TMFranklin.com.

Or for all the latest news on upcoming releases, giveaways, and exclusive content, subscribe to T.M. Franklin's newsletter at
bit.ly/TMFranklinSubscribe.

55766760R00131

Made in the USA
San Bernardino, CA
05 November 2017